THEIR LITTLE SECRETS

a twisty domestic thriller

VANESSA GARBIN

Published by The Book Folks

London, 2022

This book is a work of fiction. Names, characters, businesses, organizations, places and events are either the product of the author's imagination or are used fictitiously. Any resemblance to actual persons, living or dead, events or locales is entirely coincidental. The spelling is Australian English.

ISBN 978-1-80462-023-6

www.thebookfolks.com

Also by Vanessa Garbin

WHAT WE DID LAST NIGHT
THE LIES I TOLD HIM
YOUR EVERY MOVE
THE STEPS WE TAKE

Full details can be found at the back of this book.

www.thebookfolks.com

Prologue

She really hadn't thought things through when she responded to the direct message.

'Do you want to be my sugar baby?' he'd asked. They'd only been chatting for a few minutes.

It was exciting at first.

After she responded to the stranger with a vague 'maybe' she allowed her imagination to take flight.

She pictured herself jetting across the globe, staying at luxurious five-star hotels, draping herself in designer gowns, glittering jewels dripping from her ears.

She'd show her jerk of a boyfriend, Flynn. She'd show Sophie, her workmate, the girl Flynn had cheated on her with.

She'd show everyone.

No more making burgers and fries in a grease-coated kitchen seven days a week. She finally had a first-class boarding pass out of her shitty life.

But now, sitting on the edge of a motel bed, in a room that smells stale and strange, she is starting to regret it all.

Her entire body feels sticky and dirty in this cheap environment. Not that she is a princess or anything. She has lived her entire life in government housing. But she and her family, and most of their neighbours, are proud people, and keep their homes clean and tidy.

She wishes she could be home right now, folding laundry with her mother, something she usually complains about.

'Put this on,' orders the man, who is yet to call her by name or even meet her eyes.

He's a lot older than her. Double her age, she guesses, so… maybe forty. Or he could be just an old-looking thirty-something. He has a bland face, and rubbery-looking skin with balding pale hair.

His suit is expensive and fits well, she thinks, as she takes the dress from his outstretched hand. He smells good, rich.

Maybe this will work out. He could be testing her first, in this dump, before they move on to more lavish surroundings.

She forces a smile, but he's too busy on his phone to notice, so she takes the satin dress and the wasted smile and shuts herself in the bathroom to get changed.

The dress fits well, highlighting and exaggerating her curves but also flattering her narrow waist.

She starts to feel more confident, happier even. Until she spies a stain on the dress, just below her right hip. A white-ish smear, like dried glue.

Her stomach turns. She knows what that stain is.

Now she is repulsed, her skin crawling. Who knows how many other girls wore this thing before her?

She wants to take it off and tell the man that she's changed her mind. That she doesn't want to do this anymore.

She stares at herself in the mirror, at her long, brown hair cascading over her shoulders, at her dark, Bambi eyes, and nods her head. She can do better. So much better than this bland, rude man. There must be websites where she can find herself a proper daddy. A gentleman who knows how to treat his baby.

But something warns her, a primitive instinct deep in the base of her gut, that this man is dangerous.

She decides to keep the dirty dress on and to do whatever it is she has to do in order to get the hell out of this room. It'll be good practice anyway. She'll have to get used to sleeping with men that repulse her.

She steps out of the bathroom. The man looks at her breasts and then his eyes drop to her hips. He nods. His face is red and coated with sweat.

Her skin crawls and she can't help but shudder with disgust.

The man notices. His expression grows dark and menacing, and his eyes narrow. It turns her blood to ice and her skin breaks out in goosebumps. How can this be the same man she chatted with online? He seemed so friendly, so flirtatious and sexy.

'Now take it off and lie face down on the bed.'

She does as she is told, and while she lies there breathing through her mouth because the bedcover reeks of something unpleasant, she thinks of her younger brother and her older sister, of her parents, and of how much she loves them.

Then she thinks of her cheating boyfriend, Flynn, and wonders if he's thinking of her.

He is the last thought running through her mind before she feels a searing pain so shocking, that her world turns black.

1

Sara

It's unusual for my husband to be home for dinner. For the past few months he has been staying back at work. He normally arrives sometime after 9pm and by then I've already eaten.

'Do you like the flowers, Sara?' Edward asks, his green eyes gleaming with self-pride. 'See those yellow ones buried in the greenery there? The most expensive bloom in the shop. The florist explained to me how rare they are right now. Primrose lilacs.'

He pours himself another glass of red wine and tops up my untouched glass, then winks at me, his expression one of smugness.

My husband should know by now that rare and expensive things don't do a thing for me. I can find just as much joy in admiring a pretty weed or the clouds in the sky, and it costs me absolutely nothing.

'Yes, they are lovely,' I say, eyeing the sweet-smelling flowers nestled in the floral arrangement Edward has placed in a crystal vase on the table. 'Thank you,' I say, cutting into my steak.

It took me years to master the art of cooking expensive meat, and no matter how many times we have it for dinner, I always take great pleasure in the way my knife slices through it like butter.

Edward doesn't touch his food.

I know he's waiting to ask me something. The wine, the flowers, being home for dinner... he's setting me up to say yes to whatever it is that he wants.

'So, my parents would like us to stay over for the weekend,' he asks, before taking a huge gulp of wine. He should take it easy on that. I've noticed how ruddy his cheeks are becoming.

My fingers tighten around my cutlery.

'That sounds nice, but I've been asking you for weeks to come with me to visit my mother and you're always finding excuses. Now you suddenly have time for a whole weekend with your parents.'

Edward's face drops and he turns his head for a moment, but I can still see him roll his eyes.

'Your mother lives in a one-bedroom apartment. I can't sleep on a fold-out couch. I've been brought up in king-size beds my whole life, Sara.'

I'm tempted to say *poor you* and offer him a tissue, but instead I chew my food.

He finally slices into his steak and pops a strip of medium-rare meat into his mouth. After he finishes chewing and swallows, he shakes his head at me.

'You and I have vastly different standards of comfort, Sara. Be reasonable.'

When I first met Edward, at a soup kitchen of all places – he the volunteer server and me the grateful and very hungry receiver – he wasn't like this, full of self-importance.

In fact, I hadn't known he was from money until a month into our relationship, when he took me out to meet his parents for the first time. We spent the night at his family's luxury four-storey home, set on an acreage of walled gardens which reminded me of my favourite childhood novel, *The Secret Garden.*

To say I was wowed by the lifestyle and comfort Edward had been blessed to grow up in would be an understatement. And because I'd been estranged from my mother at the time, and living out of my car, spending my nights keeping warm in the local twenty-four-hour McDonald's, stepping into Edward's beautiful home, and into the warm embrace of his mother, was heaven-like.

So it's not that I don't wish to see his parents or visit their lovely home. Edith and Jeoffrey have always been kind towards me and treat me like a daughter. It's just that these weekend stays usually add to the pressure of what is already a highly stressful and sensitive situation Edward and I have found ourselves in.

You see, we can't have children.

I keep losing them.

My body fails to nurture our precious babies beyond the twenty-five-week mark. No matter how many different pills my obstetrician prescribes me or how well I eat or how much bed rest I get while pregnant, I always lose my babies.

The harsh truth is that I will likely never carry a baby to full term.

If you asked me two years ago what I thought about it, I'd say I'd be devastated by the fact, and likely still desperately scouring the internet for success stories on forums posted by couples like us, still holding out hope that we would one day be blessed with a noisy family of boisterous kids to raise.

But now, considering I was hospitalised after my last loss, I have accepted my fate.

Edward has not.

Which is odd because I know that all the trying has exhausted him. He has said as such many times. He has also complained that sex is boring now.

Only last weekend he was wistfully recalling the crazy amount of spontaneous sex we used to have in the first couple of years of our relationship. Those wonderful days of countertop sex and car bonnet sex.

I told him that we can go back to that. To hell with

carefully planned, cycle-dictated intercourse. Let's just go back to enjoying ourselves. Enjoy our coupledom.

We are never going to have a child of our own, is what I wanted to say, but couldn't.

But here he is, suggesting a weekend at his parents, which he knows is always loaded with questions like, 'So, Sara, any good news yet?' from my father-in-law, or looks of disappointment on my mother-in-law's face when I accept a glass of wine or eat a piece of soft cheese.

I'm not heartless though. I do feel bad for Edward's mother, Edith. Because I know her yearning for grandchildren comes from an innocent place of love and nurturing deep within her soul.

Edward's father, Jeoffrey, also seems disappointed that no grandchildren are forthcoming, and although I don't see the same warmth in his eyes as I see in Edith's when discussing the possibility of babies, the lack of grandchildren does seem to bother him. Maybe it's because Edward is their only child, and he fears the family line will die with him. Which is an understandable reason for his disappointment.

But now that I know that I'm destined to never have children of my own, I'm starting to direct my focus elsewhere. There are so many underprivileged children out there in need of help. Help that we can provide.

'I wonder...' I say, my cheeks warming at the intensity of my husband's gaze. He hardly looks at me anymore, so it's a little unsettling. 'If perhaps one weekend we could both go out and, I don't know, visit those abandoned buildings where the underprivileged kids hang out.'

Edward is quiet for a few seconds, then he makes a sound at the back of his throat.

'What? To get knifed for my wallet?' he finally says, drawing his head back theatrically at my suggestion. 'Are you crazy? Where did this come from anyway? Why are you even bringing it up?'

'I thought we could ask if any of them need our help, some food, clothing, or maybe we can help them to find proper accommodation, you know, at those safe houses. We have so much,' I say, glancing around at the sleek interior of our stunning home. 'I think we should share it with those who are not as fortunate as us.'

My husband raises his brows and curls his lips, making himself look unattractive.

'They'll only want our money for drugs. Not for food. Give me a break. Those kids are not underprivileged. They choose to be there, Sara.'

I take a sip of my wine as I regard the sneering man sitting across from me. So different to the kind face smiling down at me as he offered me the comfortingly warm pea and ham soup all those years ago. What happened to the compassionate man I fell in love with?

'Well, perhaps I'll visit the area myself during the week. There's a van that goes around, handing out food and toiletries. Nellie from the coffee shop, her husband runs it. She said they need a new volunteer.'

Edward's eyes bulge out of his head. 'Over my dead body. And put yourself and our future child's life at risk?'

I'm careful not to slam my wine glass against our polished jarrah dining table.

'What future child? I'm not pregnant, Eddie.' My throat thickens with emotion. 'In case you don't remember, I nearly bled to death last time. I just...' I trace my finger down the stem of the wine glass as I think about the fifth baby I miscarried. Due in October. Our little Libra baby. We didn't find out the sex because we didn't want to push our luck. We just wanted our baby, boy or girl, to have a chance at life. 'I don't know if I can go through that again,' I say, my voice a hoarse whisper. 'The loss, the pain... the mental and physical and emotional drain afterwards.'

As my husband watches me and listens, his face reddens.

'What? You think I haven't suffered either?' he says, after a long silence. Spit flies out of his mouth and lands on the edge of my dinner plate. 'That was the worst day of my life. I lost my unborn child and I nearly lost you.'

'I know,' I say, wiping away the dot of spit with my finger. 'Of course you've suffered. We both have.'

He swallows down something, either anger or sadness, I can't tell. I can never tell lately with Edward. He used to be so readable. Back when things were so much better between us.

I slide my hand across the table and tentatively touch his fingertips with mine. 'I don't want you to suffer any more sadness either, Eddie.'

'Thank you,' he says, his words tight and laced with bitterness. 'For thinking of me.'

His phone pings. Then it pings again.

'Do you need to check that?' I say, because I suddenly want this conversation to end. I want to eat my dinner in peace, shower and then disappear into a good book.

Usually, after he gets home from work, my husband takes his phone and disappears into the bathroom or the garage, sometimes for hours on end. Work-related, he always says, by way of explanation.

But for all I know he's having an affair with a colleague and she's burning up his phone with racy messages and nudes. I suppose that would fall into the 'work-related' category. Normally I'm annoyed by it. But right now, it's the least of my concerns.

Unfortunately, Edward strangely seems less interested by his phone tonight as he ignores the beeps and alluring notifications.

'No. I want to continue this conversation,' he says, his knuckles turning white as he makes fists and then stretches his fingers out again and rests them against the table's smooth, shiny surface.

'Are you okay?' I ask, concerned now. 'You seem so stressed out lately. Is there something you're not telling me?'

He shakes his head and exhales deeply, then drops his shoulders.

'Nothing's wrong, Sara. I just... I need to be around my family. This empty house...' His gaze wanders past me to the wall behind my back, which is adorned with our wedding photos, but sorely lacking the photos of our much-wanted babies, the imagined family we had both wished so hard for.

I sigh, slide my wine back towards me and take a sip.

'Okay. How about we visit your parents this weekend, but on the way back, we visit my mum for afternoon tea on Sunday. Deal?'

I want to add that I'll be visiting the underprivileged teens one day in the future, whether he likes it or not, but decide that what he doesn't know won't hurt him for now.

He sits and broods for a minute, before he seems to force his face into something closely resembling acceptance.

'Okay, deal,' he says.

I smile and try to inject a little humour into the dark, intense energy hovering between us.

'You didn't do it properly,' I say, grinning.

My husband's face relaxes into a genuine smile and my stomach flutters. I've forgotten how handsome Edward looks when he's not stressed to the max.

'Deal,' he says, holding out his hands in front of him and rubbing his fingers and thumbs together, like the contestants from the old television show used to do. 'There, happy now?'

I nod, then giggle. 'Yes. That's much better.'

It's as though a magic wand has been waved over us and all the tension between us dissolves. For the first time in months, we enjoy our meal together, and discuss plans for a potential trip to Europe sometime later in the year.

Then Edward manages to surprise me once again, with two slices of chocolate-caramel mousse cake from my favourite cake shop for dessert.

We take our wine into the living room afterwards, to watch some trashy reality show on the telly together, our thighs touching as we share the same couch, something we haven't done in a long while.

But the fun stops when a newsflash rolls across the bottom of the television screen.

Body sighted at Lakeland Gardens. Police divers set to begin underwater search and recovery.

My blood runs cold. Lakeland Gardens is a neighbouring suburb to ours, where our best friends, Neve and Stan, live. This is something I've been fearing for the past two weeks. Ever since Liv disappeared.

I grip Edward's warm hand for comfort. 'You don't think it's...'

My husband's face pales. 'Oh... oh God, I hope not.'

2

Sara

'Should I call Neve? Or maybe you should call Stan?'

Edward shakes his head. 'No. I think we should wait until they reach out to us.' He rubs at the furrows in his brow. 'I mean, it's not like they've said it's a teenage girl. And Liv is with friends, isn't she? There's no reason for it... for this body to be her.'

'You're right.' I sigh with relief. 'It's just a coincidence. This body could be anyone, someone from another area, a guy who got drunk or lost maybe, then fell into the water and drowned,' I say, reassuring myself and my husband with the morbid possibility.

Edward remains pale, his eyes wide, his mind buried somewhere beneath a cloud of dark fears, just like mine.

'But God, if this body... if it's her, they will never recover from this,' Edward says. He covers his mouth. 'Oh gosh, poor Jakey.'

Liv's little brother, Jake, hasn't been the same since Liv left. He refuses to go to football practice because he blames himself for Liv having left while he was at a game. He believes she would never have left home if he had been there to talk her out of it.

'But it won't be Liv. Of course it won't be,' I say, reaching for a nearby blanket and covering myself with it up to my chin. 'If something bad had happened to her after she left, her friends would have contacted Neve and Stan. Surely.'

Edward frowns.

'But what if she isn't with friends? She could have met someone online, who knows? Some forty-year-old creep posing as a teenager.'

'Oh God, don't say that.'

I stare at the television in disbelief and wait for the same words to scroll along the bottom of the screen, to make sure we haven't read it wrong. But there they are, white letters against a blue banner, flying across the base of the screen while a journalist covers a fluff story about an elderly dog who wears a top hat and tails.

My heart flutters in panic for Neve.

Even though I've never carried a child full term, I know the pain that the loss of a child brings.

And I can only imagine it magnifies after nurturing that child for over seventeen years.

My phone pings with a message, and Edward and I gasp in unison and both stare at it with wide eyes.

'Neve,' I say, before I open the message with trembling fingers.

'What did she write?'

I read the message then glance up from my phone, feeling strangely numb.

'She wants me to go over there tomorrow morning.'

Edward's eyes soften with sympathy.

'Maybe I should take a day off and be there for Stan. Because if it is Liv that they find in the water…' Edward shivers at the thought.

'It's weird, Edward,' I say, staring at the message in disbelief.

'What's weird?' He frowns at me.

'What she's written is weird.'

'What do you mean?' he says, not hiding his irritation. 'Her missing daughter could be floating around in that swamp lake. What part of her wanting you to come over to support her is weird?'

I thrust my phone at him so that he can read the message for himself.

'She's invited me over for a *champagne brunch*.'

My husband draws his head back at first, and takes in what I've said, before he leans in to read the message for himself.

'What? Does she plan on celebrating?' He shakes his head. 'I know Liv has given them hell at times, but she is their daughter.' He frowns. 'You're right. It is bloody weird.'

'I don't even want to go,' I say, dropping my phone onto the couch. 'How can anyone eat or drink while a body is floating around only a few hundred metres away?'

Edward gnaws on his thumbnail and shakes his

head.

'No. You have to go, Sars. You need to be there with her, for support. Who knows? Maybe this is just a strange reaction. She's wanting to pretend it's not happening.'

A horrible dark feeling envelopes me, making me shiver. Surely this body is not beautiful Liv. It can't be. It just can't. I refuse to believe it.

'But what if she *is* off living with friends like she told them?' I say, reassuring myself with the possibility. 'Teenagers are notorious for leaving home in a huff, aren't they? Then when they realise how hard life is they come running back.'

'Yeah, true,' says Edward.

But I can tell by the frown etched deep into his forehead that he's not buying it. I don't think I am either. Liv just isn't that type of teenager.

I recall, with a chill, the day Neve called me, sobbing on the phone to tell me that Liv had run away. Liv had left home while Neve was out watching Jake play a game of football. Stan had apparently tried to stop her, but he told Neve that no amount of pleading could convince her to stay.

I tried, too. But my messages were met with a coldness that was unfamiliar to me, with Liv's reply suggesting that she wanted nothing more to do with Edward and me, and that we needed to 'mind our own business and stop ruining other people's lives.'

I've always found that odd, her choice of wording, as though she despised us, blamed us, for whatever it was that she was going through.

It hurt, too. We have adored Liv since the day she was born. The feeling seemed mutual, too, or so I thought. I can't for the life of me think of anything we may have done to have changed the way she feels about us.

Edward's phone pings from the kitchen and he

excuses himself to go check his notifications. The kitchen door, which opens to the garage, shuts, and I know that he's back to his usual routine, his 'work-related' stuff.

After I message Neve, telling her that I'll be there tomorrow, I take a shower and lather up with the new lavender-scented body wash I purchased this morning, hoping that it'll relax me enough to be able to sleep tonight.

I'm usually fast asleep by the time Edward joins me in bed, after he's spent a good two hours doing whatever it is he gets up to in the garage.

But tonight, after the news flash across the bottom of the television screen, and Neve's bizarre invitation, I don't think I'll be able to sleep at all.

3

Sara

I'm woken by Edward calling my name and shaking me by my shoulder.

'Sara. Wake up,' he hisses.

'What?'

I blink several times, wondering why the room is so bright, and ease myself into a sitting position.

Edward exhales through his nostrils and takes a bit of time to speak. He's still wearing his pyjama shorts and his blond hair is sticking out in all directions.

The mattress squeaks when he sits down.

It's not until he puts his phone on my lap that I remember why I had such a restless sleep last night.

That news flash across the bottom of the television screen.

I shiver.

Just knowing that a dead body is only a short car ride away from our house turns my blood cold.

Edward rubs his face then clears his throat.

'They found the body. Female, between fifteen and twenty-five years of age. No identity yet.' He gestures to his phone which still rests on my lap. 'It's all in the article.'

'Oh my God, Eddie,' I say, reaching out to grab hold of his arm for just a moment.

'I know,' he says gravely.

I take the phone and read the news story. After I've finished, I notice the time. It's 8.30am. I never sleep beyond 7am, even on a Sunday.

'Did you take the day off?'

He nods.

'Why did you let me sleep in so late?' I turn and swipe my phone off the bedside table. 'My alarm should have woken me.'

'I turned it off. You need your rest. Remember what the doctor said.'

'That was three months ago,' I say, unable to hide the irritation in my voice. The time for Edward treating me like I'm a delicate flower is over. 'The doctor told me to take it easy, he didn't tell me to wrap myself in cotton wool.'

Edward shrugs. 'You're always so wound up. I thought a good rest would... help.'

'Well, I'm done resting. And you know I hate sleeping in.' I shake my head. 'Of all the mornings,' I mutter to myself, as I toss the covers aside and get out of bed and head straight for my wardrobe.

'I'm sorry,' he says, rising to his feet, clearly offended

going by the look on his face.

'I'm going straight to Neve's,' I say, my throat raspy. Despite the lavender shower gel I used, I hardly slept a wink last night, and only fell asleep when dawn birds started warbling outside our bedroom window. Every time I closed my eyes, I saw dark waters and bloated dead bodies.

'I'm coming too,' he says, joining me inside the walk-in wardrobe. 'Stan will be... shit, it'll be hell for him, hell for them both. God, it's torturous enough for us and she's not even our daughter.'

My husband's anxious words soften me towards him. He loves Liv as much as I do. He's always adored her.

'How long do you think it'll take to identify the body?' I ask, unable to repress the full body shiver that rattles my bones.

Edward sucks in a sharp breath. 'I'm not sure. Not long I would expect. It helps if the person has already been reported missing or a family member comes forward to the police,' he says, quickly choosing a pair of grey slacks, a white cotton shirt and an emerald-green jumper to throw over the top of it. Green has always been Edward's colour, and the emerald perfectly matches his uniquely coloured eyes.

'I feel awful for hoping that it's someone else, that it's not Liv they've found,' I say, grabbing a pair of leggings, a cream-coloured ribbed top and a long, light brown cardigan. 'Because whoever she is, she's someone's daughter, someone's sister or friend. This is devastating, no matter who it is.'

Edward shivers. 'I'm going to have a quick shower,' he says.

'Don't be too long,' I call out, tapping out a quick text to Neve, letting her know that I'm coming early before I toss my phone onto the bed. 'And leave it running for me when you're finished.'

'Yep,' he says, as he disappears into the en-suite

bathroom.

I listen to the pipes whine and the water groan within the walls. It's become such a familiar sound over the past few months that I keep forgetting it's a problem.

I mention it to Edward, five minutes later, as he emerges from the bathroom with a towel draped around his damp body.

'We need to get the plumbing checked out. There's water leaking into the wall of the spare bedroom. We might end up with structural damage if we leave it too late.'

My husband's face pales a little at first before his cheeks turn pink, as though he's embarrassed that our stunning home is less than perfect.

'I've got it sorted,' he says, giving me a thumbs up without meeting my gaze. 'It's a busy time for plumbers. The last one I called said there's a three-month wait time for call-outs.'

Hmmm. I want to tell him that Neve called a plumber to her house last week, for a leak in the toilet that I pointed out while I was visiting. The man arrived within fifteen minutes and had the job done in less than that time.

But I decide to leave it.

It is strange though. It's not like we don't have any money. Well, we have separate bank accounts, so I don't know how much Edward has in his own account exactly. But from memory, when I accidentally opened one of his bank statements that came through the post last year, it's a lot. As in, seven-figures a lot.

Edward is always telling me that I never have to work again. But since taking my long-service leave, three months ago, after my last miscarriage, I've been itching to return to work. Perhaps not to the same job as a medical receptionist, though, because since I've had time away from my desk, I've reconsidered my options.

But I'd like to occupy my days doing *something* of worth.

Lately I've been thinking about a change of career. Something involving working with kids. Kids that are either doing it tough on the street or simply struggling with their low-level income families and in need of support, support that I can provide.

Maybe I can ask Stan about his homeless charity organisation. See if he needs any volunteers. I would be helping people and gaining much needed experience at the same time.

Eventually I'd like to start something up on my own, a community service which would focus on children and teens in need. But for now, helping anyone who needs it would be great. And it would be amazing to give back to Stan's charity, to volunteer at the very place I received soup and sanctuary while I was homeless so many years ago.

Of course, I won't be asking Stan today. It wouldn't be right. But sometime in the future I will.

'The shower's running,' Edward says, waving a hand in front of my face, ushering me back into the present.

'Oh, okay, thanks.'

After we're both showered and dressed, we grab our phones and whatever else we need and soon we are in our cars reversing out the driveway.

Edward insisted on taking his own car in case he needs to leave for work at short notice. Odd considering he's taken the complete day off. But, then again, he's not immune to getting called out on weekends so it's not like it would be a complete surprise if he was called away at some stage today on his day off.

Either way I'm glad. I enjoy being alone in my Mustang. Driving puts me in the present moment and helps me to clear my head. And the low rumble of all eight cylinders soothes my nerves as I drive to Neve's.

Their house is only a few minutes away from ours, but due to certain roads being cordoned off by the police while the Lakeland Gardens waters are being searched, I take the long, winding way there for which I'm grateful. It gives me enough time to compose myself and emotionally prepare for what may eventuate today.

'Please don't be Liv,' I whisper to myself as several police cars overtake me, making my stomach churn and my head light.

Beautiful Liv. The girl whom I've watched grow from a tiny, screaming newborn, through the chubby, cheeky toddler years, and all the way to the gorgeous, intelligent, and feisty young woman who throws her arms in the air and squeals with excitement whenever she sees me. Liv is the closest I've ever come to having a daughter in my life.

Tears prickle my eyes and I blink them away.

It's only been a fortnight, but I miss Liv so much already. We all do. And we desperately want her to come home.

By the time I pull into Neve's drive, I'm a trembling, emotional wreck. So much for composing myself on the way over.

All I want to do is put my car in reverse and get the hell out of here. Pretend that all is well. Forget that a young woman's body has been found only a few hundred metres from Neve and Stan's place.

But in the end, I force my body to do what it doesn't want to and get out of my car.

Low grey clouds have gathered, obscuring the blue sky and sunshine that had been visible from my bedroom window when I woke this morning. It's as though the sky is preparing itself to mourn.

I'm surprised to see that Edward's and my own car are the only two in the driveway. There is a car parked along the verge, but it may belong to one of the neighbours. I'd imagined the police and perhaps the press camping out in the front yard. But then I remind myself that the rest of the world doesn't know that Liv is missing.

I recall Neve telling me how she'd had a huge fight with Stan after she called the police to declare Liv missing the day she left. How he'd embarrassed her when the police showed up at the front door, apologising to the officers, telling them that Neve was overreacting, and that Liv was perfectly fine and staying with friends.

But what if she's not fine?

What if...

I shiver at the thought.

No, I tell myself. Stop thinking the worst.

My stomach is a knotted mess while I wait with Edward at the front door.

Now I feel unsure. I should have waited until Neve had responded to my message before we showed up like this on their doorstep, two hours earlier than she was expecting me to arrive for the champagne brunch she'd invited only *me* to.

Edward takes my hand in his and I cling to the security of his hold, his touch. I'm certain he feels as anxious as I do because his fingers squeeze mine and he inhales sharply when we hear footsteps from inside approaching the door.

The door opens and Neve blinks in surprise when she sees us.

'I sent a text,' I say.

'Oh, I haven't been on my phone,' says Neve, frowning, but then brightens when she shifts her gaze to Edward. 'Stan,' she calls over her shoulder as she unlocks the security screen door. 'Eddie's here,' she says in a sing-song voice.

She steps aside to allow us both to enter the cool, marble hallway of their home, the familiar scent of ylang-ylang wafting over us.

Everything appears normal. The house too clean, Neve's makeup too perfect, her expression too nonchalant for my liking.

But who am I to judge? I'm not a parent and I've never been in the same situation as Neve so I can hardly put myself in her shoes. Neve's obviously trying hard to push aside the possibility of the body being Liv. It's her way of coping. I'm sure any mother would do the same.

'Neve,' I say, wanting to wrap my arms around my tiny friend. 'Have you heard anything?'

Neve takes a step back. Her eyes, which have dark shadows beneath them, shift away for a split second before she meets my gaze again and waves an admonishing hand at me.

'Tonnes of people go missing every day.' She shrugs. 'It's a perfectly normal day for us.'

Edward glances at me from the corner of his eye and raises his brow ever so slightly. He's just as confused and as alarmed as I am.

'But why is Stan home?' Edward asks.

Neve shrugs. 'He just wanted a day off. You know. Have a bludge day.' She smiles at my husband, batting her false lashes at him playfully. 'You two boys should get a game of golf in this afternoon. I'm sure Stan would love that.'

'What's this?' says Stan, materialising in the hallway, a wide grin on his face to see us both.

He shuffles up to Edward, boxer-like, and lightly punches his arm, then leans forward to gently plant a peck on my cheek. He smells fresh, like limes, and his hair is damp.

'Did you get the sack from your old man?' he asks Edward with a laugh.

Edward stiffens at Stan's remark and doesn't smile back. 'I came with Sara… in case… well, for support.'

Stan sighs deeply and pats Edward's shoulder. 'Thanks, mate.' He then meets my gaze, and his blue eyes grow shiny with emotion. 'We are so lucky to have friends like you two.'

Neve shuffles closer to Stan's side and slips her arm around his waist. She looks like a child standing beside her tall husband.

'Maybe we should tell them,' Neve says with a heavy sigh. She brushes a strand of hair behind her ear, and I notice the tremor in her hand.

'Tell us what?' Edward asks.

'There's something Neve and I have kept from you both,' says Stan, rubbing the back of his neck. 'Something we should have told you last week.'

4

Sara

Edward slides his hand around my waist and draws me to his side. I can tell that he's just as anxious as I am to hear what Stan has to say.

'I heard from Liv last week,' says Stan, glancing down at Neve.

'She's still not talking to me,' Neve says, her hand fluttering to her throat.

'Liv's in Melbourne, staying with friends. She has a job in a supermarket of all places,' Stan says, his gaze fixed to the marble floor tiles. When he looks up, he has tears in his eyes.

Neve blinks back her own tears as she watches her husband well up with emotion.

'While we are horrified and so sad that a young woman's body has been found, we are also grateful that it's not our daughter,' she says. 'That our Liv is alive and well.'

Stan clears his throat and sighs, shaking his head as though he wants to say something but can't, due to his heightened emotions.

Neve dabs at her eyes with her fingertips and steps forward, her pale cheeks flushed pink. She takes both my hands in hers and holds them tight.

'So please forgive us,' she says, smiling through her tears, 'for wanting to celebrate the fact that our daughter is alive.'

I stare at Neve's pretty face, unsure what to feel while I take in what she and Stan have just told us. But then I finally exhale and force myself to say something.

'Oh my gosh, Neve. Stan. That's wonderful news. Thank God Liv is okay.'

Conflicting emotions clash inside of me. I'm happy, but angry.

And so confused.

I sneak a glance at Edward, and he widens his eyes ever so slightly in understanding.

'But I wish you could have told us,' I say. 'We've been worried sick since she left. And ever since we saw the news last night it's been...'

'Hell,' Edward finishes for me. He feels just as deeply about Neve and Stan's kids as I do.

Stan grimaces. 'I'm sorry. We should have told you both.' He slaps his own hand. 'Naughty, naughty.' Then he grins at us, his tears gone. 'Can I make amends by cracking open a bottle of Bollinger?'

Edward looks at me, his face softening into a 'if you can't beat 'em, join 'em' kind of smile while he lightly shrugs his shoulders. 'Well, it is Friday...'

I force a smile, surprised at how quickly the mood has changed. A dead girl has been found only a short walk from this house, and now we're back to light-hearted banter between friends.

'Okay, bubbly is a good start,' I say, before raising my brows at Stan. 'But you're not entirely off the hook.'

He roars with laughter and disappears into the kitchen. Edward follows him and leaves Neve and me alone in the hallway.

'Let's all sit in the alfresco together,' she says, lightly touching my arm. 'I ordered in the cutest little frittatas from that new café in the city. Have you eaten?'

'No,' I say, the mention of food bringing my stomach back to life with a growl. I cover my belly in embarrassment. 'We literally woke up, showered, dressed and came here right away.'

'Oh, you poor darlings,' Neve says, her face turning serious. 'I knew I should have told you we'd finally heard from Liv. But I was worried you'd message her right away and then she'd think I was telling everyone her business. You know how private she is. And she's not even talking to me yet. I don't need her to find another reason to be angry with me.'

I nod in understanding.

'Does Stan know why Liv's not talking to you?'

'Yeah, he said he has a good idea why.' Neve raises her eyebrows. 'He also said he can't betray her trust, but he made her promise she'll give me a call one day when she's ready to talk.' She shrugs. 'It's better than nothing, I suppose. But it's so frustrating, you know? Having Stan as some kind of... gatekeeper to my own daughter. I hate it.'

I nod. There's so much I want to say right now, because so much of this doesn't sit right with me. But for now, I think it's best to leave things be. Neve doesn't need the added stress. And anyway, I want to talk things over with Edward first, and see what he thinks. I need to make sure I'm not overthinking everything and getting myself into a state of paranoia.

'Let's go check on the boys, make sure they've saved us some bubbly,' says Neve grinning. 'And then you three can sit outside while I prepare the frittatas. You okay with dressed rocket and orange slices on the side?'

'Of course,' I say, but my mind is still on Liv and the nameless body which has been dragged from the water only two streets away from here.

Goosebumps prickle my forearms. Something is most definitely off about this whole situation... and I can't be the only one who thinks it.

When we enter the kitchen, Stan flinches and quickly slips his phone into his back pocket. Edward is nowhere to be found.

'Where's Eddie?' asks Neve.

Stan's face reddens. He flicks a glance at the kitchen window, avoiding eye contact. 'I think he's gone to sit outside already.'

The air in the kitchen is intense. Stan's hair looks as though it's been ruffled, and his shirt seems crumpled at the neck. A bottle of Bollinger sits on the countertop unopened.

'Did you lose a button?' I ask, noticing the open neck of Stan's shirt. He is nearly always immaculately dressed and I'm almost one hundred percent sure that he did not have a button missing a minute ago.

Stan brushes his hands down his front.

'Oh.' He looks at Neve. 'I thought you threw this one out, hon?'

'Why would you throw it out?' I say. 'It only takes a needle and thread, and it'll be as good as new.'

It never fails to amuse me how frivolous wealthy people are with their belongings. Even though I've got plenty of money now, I can't help but mend the holes in my socks, much to Edward's amusement.

Neve and Stan stare at me like I've grown an extra head.

'I suppose,' says Neve, shrugging her shoulders. 'But who can be bothered fiddling with all of that when you can just walk into a shop and buy another shirt?'

Something clangs outside.

'That's the side gate,' says Neve, glancing up sharply at Stan.

He shrugs and looks away.

At the unmistakable sound of my husband's car starting – the bone-rattling rumble a result of the modified exhaust Edward had installed a few months ago – Stan locks eyes with mine for a split second.

'Why would Eddie leave?' asks Neve.

Stan looks at her with wide eyes, before shrugging again, suggesting he knows nothing.

I open my mouth to speak but the sound of a door slamming shut interrupts me. The back door by the sounds of it. And a few seconds later a man enters the room, his fingers and clothes covered in blue and green paint. He has fair hair, and looks a bit like Stan, but judging by the extra crow's feet around his eyes, is a few years older. Stan and Neve don't seem at all bothered by the fact that this dishevelled person has just waltzed into their home as though he lives here.

Stan smiles at me and pats the man's back.

'Sara, meet my brother Lawrence. He's staying with us for a while, in our back shed, until he gets back onto his feet.'

For a moment I'm stunned. I'd always heard about Stan's reclusive artist brother who'd become estranged from his parents many years ago. But I've never actually met him. And I find it odd that Neve hadn't mentioned the fact that Lawrence has come to stay. But then again, Liv hasn't been gone long so I can hardly expect Neve to be keeping me in the loop with everything going on in her life while her mind is consumed with her runaway daughter.

'I think I left my car keys here somewhere,' Lawrence says, ignoring me.

Neve reaches into the nearby fruit bowl. 'Here they are. You left them on the counter last night.'

'Thanks.' He takes them from Neve and stuffs them into the pocket of his torn jeans.

He turns to leave, still not acknowledging my existence, but he pauses, his back to us all. 'Your friend didn't look happy when he left, Stan. What did you two argue about?'

Stan doesn't respond.

In silence, we all watch Lawrence disappear down the hallway. The sound of the back door slamming shut jolts me out of my stupor.

Edward!

I leave the kitchen and race down the hallway to the front door. But by the time I run out of the house and up the driveway, my husband is gone.

A middle-aged woman across the street stares at me over the rims of her designer sunglasses and smirks, before getting into her car and driving away.

'Who is that?' I ask Neve.

'Oh, just our nosy neighbour. She loves drama, the wrinkly old bag. She's on her fifth facelift. One day she's not going to have any skin left to stretch. Don't worry about her.'

'Oh let it rest, Neve. Leave Sondra alone,' says Stan.

Neve folds her arms over her chest and rolls her eyes at me.

'What happened between you and Eddie?' I ask Stan, who is bending forward to pluck at the thin weeds poking through the thick, dark mulch between the rose bushes.

'God, what am I paying the bloody gardener for?' he says, ignoring my question.

'Stan,' Neve asks, frowning at him, 'are you listening? Sara's asked you a question and I want to know the answer as well. What on earth happened in the kitchen earlier? Why did Eddie leave like that? Without saying goodbye?'

Stan gives Neve a look that cools the blood in my

veins, and I shiver.

I've never seen Stan like this, so cold and angry. He's always so jovial and light-hearted. It's usually Stan having a dig at Edward to loosen up. Maybe the discovery of the young woman's body has shaken Stan more than he wants to let on.

'Look, it doesn't matter,' I say, waving my hand in the air, not wanting to cause my friends any more distress than they are already under. Plus, I'd rather find out what happened via Edward.

I look at them each in turn.

'I'm sorry. It was rude of us to turn up like this unannounced, and so early. It's such a strange time... for everyone.' I shrug, unsure of what else to say. I'm dying to slip into the cool, leather interior of my car and speed away from this house.

Stan shrugs back at me. He is sweating so hard that his shirt has grown damp at his chest and armpits.

'What do you mean?' he asks. 'It's not a strange time at all. Today is a normal day as far as I'm concerned,' he says, a hint of ice in his voice.

The back of my neck prickles.

'Okay. Well, I'm going. Sorry I can't stay. But I think I should check on my husband.' I flick a glance at Neve and soften my gaze. 'I'll call you. Take care.'

'Will do,' she says, giving me a knowing look.

I release the biggest sigh of relief as I slide into my car and start the engine.

I'm about to put my car into reverse when Lawrence emerges from the side gate of the house and crosses the lawn, still covered in paint.

He gets into his car, which is the forest green one parked on the verge I noticed earlier when we first arrived, and just before he drives away, he raises his head and stares directly at me. My car windows are tinted quite dark, so I'm not sure that Lawrence can see me very clearly, but the coldness in his gaze gives me the chills.

Stan waves at his brother then comes to stand behind Neve, and wraps his arms around her delicate shoulders, eyeballing me as I reverse out the driveway. He resembles a spider ready to drain the life out of its victim. I'm not sure what's gotten into Stan today. Or my husband. Maybe something happened with Stan's creepy brother. Who knows?

But I intend to find out.

On the way home I stop for fuel, and after I pull out of the petrol station and wait at the next set of lights, a familiar and youthful face smiles at me through my windscreen before his image blurs under a spray of detergent and water. After a few strokes with a window squeegee to wipe it all away, my window is sparkling clean.

I press the automatic button and my window glides down halfway.

'Thank you, Harley,' I say, smiling up at the dark-haired teenage boy whom I've come to know because of his window-washing gig. 'Shouldn't you be at school? I thought this was just a weekend thing.'

Harley slips the ten-dollar note I hand him into his back pocket and then tucks a lock of his raven hair behind his ear.

'Thanks for the ten bucks, Sara.' He eyes the police van on the opposite side of the road and slides his backpack over his shoulder. 'Gotta run,' he says, before he pulls his cap down low and darts across the road, disappearing down a lane between two blocks of apartments.

Kids like Harley are why I want to start volunteering. Edward is so obsessed with bringing another child into the world, but there are so many already here with us who are in need.

The lights turn green, and as I put my foot down, I turn up the radio. An old eighties song is playing and for a minute or so the nostalgia of the tune relaxes me and reminds me of the better part of my childhood, the time when it was just me and Mum facing the world like a team – before she started to date creeps and users.

It's going to be so good to see her on Sunday. It'll be good for Edward to see his family again, too. Good for us both.

And if we manage to enjoy ourselves and unwind a little, maybe I'll feel confident enough to explain to Edward, in concrete terms, that I don't ever want to fall pregnant again. Ever. That I've made peace with the fact that I can't carry a baby to full term. That I've found something new to focus on – helping underprivileged kids.

But first things first.

Before I can relax and enjoy this weekend away, I need to find out what happened between my husband and Stan today.

I also need to ask Edward what he's been hiding from me. Because for the past few months, he most certainly has not been himself.

And I'm positive it has to do with that pinging phone of his.

5

Neve

'Sit down, Neve. I've boiled the kettle. Come on. It's been a while since we've had a good chat,' says my mum as she takes two of her favourite teacups and saucers out from the credenza. 'You're always so... restless lately,' she adds pointedly. 'It's aging you.'

My mother can't do subtle. I draw in a deep breath and perch myself on a stool at the kitchen bench, ready for her interrogation.

'I can't stay long, Mum. I've got to pick up Jake,' I say, giving myself an excuse should her questions become too invasive.

Mum peers at me over the rims of her spectacles. 'Doesn't Jake do the environmental club on Friday afternoons? You won't have to pick him up for at least another hour.'

'Oh, that's right,' I say, but my mother is no fool. She quirks an eyebrow and concentrates on making tea.

While she jiggles teabags, I try to mentally prepare myself for the questions she'll be asking. I'm almost certain she'll ask me about Liv again. She always does. Mum doesn't get it that I think of Liv every second of the day. Worry about her, fret about her. And every time someone else asks me where she is, it only serves to heighten my fears and deepen the pain I already feel.

Because I don't know.

I'm Liv's mother. And yet I don't know where she is.

Sure, Stan heard from Liv and tells me that she's in Melbourne. But that's not good enough.

I need to hear it from Liv, in her own words, in her own voice.

Because I know my own daughter.

And I know she wouldn't leave without saying goodbye. She loves Jakey too much. Something must have happened to have caused her to flee like that. And the fact that she reached out to Stan, and not me, means that she's upset with me for some reason.

I spend the better part of each day trying to work out what.

Liv and I have clashed quite a bit during her teenage

years, but that's only because I'm the one who gives her rules and curfews, whereas Stan is always nagging at me, on Liv's behalf, to go easy on her.

But I worry for her, that's all. Life is a jungle out there. I can't help but feel protective of our precious daughter.

Though I wonder if my overprotectiveness has pushed her away.

Perhaps I smothered my daughter to the point she couldn't breathe and needed to leave.

Every time I beg Stan to call Liv and ask her why she won't speak to me he gets angry and threatens to stop telling me anything. He thinks that I'm heading for a nervous breakdown with all 'this worrying' and that Liv needs to know that she has a stable house to return to should she suddenly change her mind and want to come home. And I suppose he's right. Stan loves Liv as much as I do. If something was terribly wrong, or if our daughter was in danger of any kind, he'd tell me. I just need to trust him on this.

'So, have you heard from Liv?' says Mum, as she slides my teacup and saucer towards me. She removes her reading glasses and sets them aside and blinks at me while she takes her tea standing up, directly across from me.

'Yes,' I say. 'She messaged to say that she's in Melbourne and doing fine. Working at a supermarket,' I say, making a face, pretending it's all okay and very normal. The last thing I want to do is worry my mother. 'Some of her friends are backpacking around Europe already, and a couple of them are working as nannies in London. Most kids fly the nest once they graduate from high school, Mum.'

Mum frowns. 'Yes, well, I know that from experience, don't I?' She gives me a knowing look and I roll my eyes. She's referring to the fact that I left home at seventeen, to go and live with my first boyfriend for all of two weeks. 'Well, tell her to respond to my messages, please. It's very unlike Liv not to write back.'

Fear stabs at my heart. I hadn't wanted to ask Mum if Liv had been responding to her messages, because to be honest, I was terrified of hearing this very thing. Why on earth would my daughter, who loves her nana, stop writing to her?

Why, Liv? Why?

'And how are things with you and Stan?' Mum asks, tucking a lock of bright red hair behind her ear. Sometime last year, my mother decided to start colouring her greys in loud colours. 'It's all the rage,' she'd said, when she first dyed her hair turquoise. 'I follow this woman called *Unicorn Granny* on Instagram,' she'd said by way of explanation, 'such an inspiration.'

'We're great,' I lie, and take a huge gulp of tea so that I don't have to say any more about my marriage.

'So has the sex gotten better?'

'Mum!'

'Sorry, but I remember you mentioning it at New Year's...'

'That was a private conversation I was having with Sara, Mum. You shouldn't have been listening in,' I say, my face warm. The last person I want to discuss my sex life with is my mother.

'Okay, okay. I'm sorry. But you don't seem as... I don't know, as enamoured with Stan as you used to be.'

'Gosh, Mum, you remember what it's like, with the stress of raising a family. Romance goes on the backburner.'

'Not for me and my Norman,' she says, her eyes twinkling. 'We always found a way to keep things romantic.'

My heart softens. Mum and Dad did truly have a magical relationship. The only couple that I've ever known to personify the term 'soulmates'.

'What you and Dad had was super special, Mum,' I

say. 'You were so lucky.'

Mum nods and wipes at her eyes, smearing her mascara. Dad's been gone for over five years now, but I don't believe my mother will ever heal from the loss.

I wish Dad were here now. Liv had such a special bond with him. He would have talked her into coming back by now, I just know it.

'But you still love Stan, don't you, darling?' Mum asks.

Unfortunately I hesitate for a second too long and Mum widens her eyes.

'Oh, Neve... you're not... you're not having an affair, are you?'

'Of course not, Mum.' I frown at her. 'How could you think that?' I shake my head. 'We've just got a lot on right now. Lawrence is still with us. I honestly thought he'd be gone by now, but Stan feels sorry for him. Says he has mental issues, so we need to be kind to him.' I straighten my spine as a shiver travels down my back. 'But he's so creepy. I just want him gone. He's always staring at me. And he looks at Stan like he hates him and yet Stan walks around bragging about Lawrence like he's brother of the year. It's just so odd.'

Mum shrugs, but her eyes seem to darken with concern as she drinks the remainder of her tea in silence.

I push Lawrence out of my mind – he's the least of our worries – and focus on Stan. On our relationship and what it's come to.

I think about the thing we did last month.

Is it a normal thing for husbands and wives to do together?

Shuddering at the memory, I bring my teacup to my lips.

But this tea is much like my relationship with Stan right now.

Cold and bitter.

6

Sara

Endless green pastures, dotted with cows and recently shorn sheep, stretch out on either side of us as we cruise the open road towards my in-laws' place. Spring wildflowers decorate the roadside in an explosion of colour, perfectly complementing all the greenery. The endless blue sky above us makes it picture perfect.

I reach out and lightly brush my fingers over the back of my husband's hand, the coarse hairs growing there tickling my fingertips.

'For all the whinging I do, I actually love the drive out to your parents' place. I mean, I don't love the lectures they give me about my biological clock ticking, but this scenery, the fresh air…'

I breathe in deep, as though I'm outside sniffing wildflowers and not breathing in the leathery scent of Edward's car.

'Yeah,' Edward says, sounding absent, as though his mind is elsewhere.

'It's like therapy. I honestly feel as though all our problems have been left behind,' I add, trying my best to goad him into conversation. There is so much I want to discuss, but it's going to be like extracting teeth if Edward doesn't start talking.

Edward keeps his eyes fixed on the road, despite his phone pinging at regular intervals from the pocket of his shirt.

'At least, temporarily,' I add, alluding to the annoying notifications.

My husband makes a sound in his throat, which could be in protest or agreement.

'Are you feeling relaxed?' I ask him. With sweat beading on his forehead, he looks anything but. 'I thought you were looking forward to seeing your mum and dad?'

He frowns and sighs. 'Of course I am. But you know how they get sometimes. I think you got into my head. Now I'm expecting all this pressure from them and you're... you know, I'm sensing that you're not...' He shakes his head and doesn't finish the sentence. 'Anyway, it's going to be tough, tougher than I realised.'

I think about what happened between my husband and Stan yesterday, how I'm still none the wiser about what occurred between them. Edward was conveniently called out for a 'work emergency' immediately after and returned home late, so we didn't get a chance to talk about it.

'Look, whatever we face, we'll face it together,' I say, patting his hand.

He's quiet for a moment, then he glances at me briefly before fixing his gaze on the endless road again.

'You mean you'll still consider... the future... potential family plans?' he asks, not bothering to hide the desperation in his voice.

It's awful of me to do this, to get my husband's hopes up, but in order to get to the bottom of what's bothering him, I decide to be agreeable. At least for the time being.

'Yes, I'm open to discussion, of course.'

My husband visibly relaxes, his shoulders sinking, his chest falling as he exhales noisily.

'Thank you, Sara. Oh God, thank you.' He grips my hand, draws it to his lips and kisses my knuckles with such passion my lower belly flutters.

Now that my husband has warmed up a little, I decide to ask him about Stan.

'So what happened between you and Stan yesterday? You left so suddenly. And Stan was all messed up and had a button missing from his shirt. It was weird.'

Edward sighs heavily, then releases my hand to turn down the classical music station he likes to listen to.

'Okay. Well, we were just chatting... and I told him how glad I am that Liv has been in touch. And then he just... he just started acting strangely.'

'In what way?' I ask, while my husband gnaws on his bottom lip. My husband has attractive lips. Pouty. Kissable lips. I hope we get to rekindle our romance during this weekend away.

After the last loss, and my stint in hospital, Edward has been hesitant to initiate sex. I think he wants to give my body a rest. But even what I've initiated hasn't exactly been romantic. Sex has become a quick, tension reliever at most. At least it's a change from the 'boring' sex Edward usually complains about while we're trying to conceive.

'Stan told me to fuck off, to stop talking about Liv. And he wouldn't look me in the eye.' Edward gnaws on his bottom lip again. 'And it made me wonder... have they really heard from Liv? Or were they just saying so? So I asked him that.'

'You asked if they were *lying*?' I put a hand to my mouth, shocked, even though I had secret reservations about their story myself.

Maybe it's because I like to think that Liv would have texted me, too, to let me know that she's okay. Because I know that girl, she's a sweet soul, and I'm certain she would reach out, if only to say that she's safe and well.

I also can't pretend that I haven't felt something, a dark feeling, gnawing in the base of my gut ever since Liv suddenly left home. And Stan and Neve are always cagey whenever Liv is mentioned, which of course feeds my suspicions.

'Yeah, I did,' says Edward, yanking me back into the present. 'And he took a swing at me. I dodged it and got him in a headlock and held him like that until he settled down. Then I let him go and bolted out the sliding door to the alfresco. I thought I'd go out there to cool down for a bit. But not long after, I left out the side gate. I just had to get out of there. I don't think Stan and I have ever had a fight before. It was... strange. I hated it.'

'Wow,' is all I can think to say. I'd half-expected Edward to brush my inquiries away. He's been so secretive lately. But instead, he's opening right up to me.

A warm feeling stirs in my chest. Because I know that my husband is telling the truth. It's an instinct. A gut feeling. Something I've learnt from listening to my mother lie throughout my later teenage years, telling me that she was 'okay' when she clearly was not.

'He'll probably hate me forever. He said he was going to call my father.'

'Call your dad?' I make a face. 'Really? What a dobber. He's a grown man, not a five-year-old. Unbelievable. Did you see his brother in the yard? Apparently, he's staying in the back shed until he gets back on his feet.'

Edward raises his brows. 'Lawrence? No. I didn't see him. Stan didn't say a word.'

'Well I met him and... he seems kind of weird.'

Edward smiles knowingly and nods his head. 'Yep, that's Lawrence. He's always been a bit of a loner. But he's not a bad sort. He's got a kind heart. He's different, that's all. It's a shame he doesn't speak with his parents anymore.'

'Yeah. That is a shame.'

I place my hand over Edward's again, the warm feeling in my heart growing. He's such a kind soul. And we're a team again, my husband and me. But it's sad and screwed up that the discovery of a dead body has brought us together.

I shiver and try to focus on the pretty purple wildflowers decorating the road's edge like twin ribbons of colour.

But Liv comes to mind again, and that familiar cold feeling creeps its way into my chest and steals away the warmth.

'Do you honestly believe that Liv is okay?' I ask.

'I'm not sure. I think you should keep messaging her, though. Until she responds,' says Edward.

'Will do,' I say, setting a mental reminder to text her later tonight.

'Good.'

My husband's phone continues to ping, until he reaches into his shirt pocket after which it falls silent.

Though I'd intended on asking about his phone and those notifications, the timing doesn't feel right. Edward has bared enough of his heart for one day. I'll leave it until tomorrow.

Edward turns up the music.

Something exceptionally beautiful is playing.

We don't speak for a while. We don't need to. The music floats between us. It's achingly lovely. The kind of music that makes you want to cry, but uplifts you at the same time, giving you hope.

'This has to be Frederick Septimus Kelly,' I guess. 'You listen to this at home on YouTube.'

My husband nods. He looks impressed and perhaps flattered that I still notice what he listens to.

'You're getting better,' he jokes.

It's a little game we play whenever we're in his car together. I never listened to classical music until I met Edward, and he used to laugh at my inability to distinguish one composer from another.

Half an hour later, we're idling in front of a grand set of iron gates. They glide open after Edward punches a code into the electronic keypad attached to the high, red-brick wall which surrounds the seven-hectare property.

I open my window and breathe in the earthy, fragrant air filled with the fresh scent of spring's wildflower blooms as well as the grassy, zesty scent of the surrounding, native bushland. Then, as we enter the walled property and travel the long driveway towards Edward's magnificent family home, the air turns sweeter with the heavily scented fragrance of the many rose blooms which grow on either side.

My stomach flutters as it always does, no matter how many times I've visited my in-laws, Mr and Mrs Kingston.

I run my damp palms down the fabric of my expensive maxi dress, smoothing it against my thighs, then sit up straight and adjust my cardigan so that it settles evenly over my shoulders.

'You look fine. Honestly,' says Edward, rolling his eyes. But he doesn't understand what it's like, growing up wearing hand-me-downs and having the kids at school turn their noses up at me because of it.

Though I've gained a mountain of self-confidence since those days, for some reason a visit to Edward's parents always seems to strip me back down to the insecure little girl I'd once been. Not that they don't make me feel welcome, they always have. It's more me. I'm my own worst enemy. The little negative voice inside of me seems to grow louder whenever I'm inside the Kingstons' opulent home, telling me that I don't belong here.

By the time we gather our things from the boot of Edward's car, and ring the front doorbell, I've managed to mute that little voice and find that I'm looking forward to a weekend of delicious meals and good conversation.

Pressure to give them grandchildren aside, Jeoffrey and Edith are great company, and always have a bucketload of fabulous travel stories to entertain us with. But I cross my fingers that they'll leave the subject of pregnancy alone this weekend.

'Welcome home, welcome home!' Edith beams as she steps back to allow us entry through the double doors.

As soon as I've set down my bags in the tiled hallway, she opens her arms to embrace me, and I'm swept up in a soft cloud of silk and Elizabeth Taylor's White Diamonds perfume. Edith once told me she hasn't changed her perfume for over thirty years, since the day Elizabeth Taylor released the scent.

'Let me look at you,' she says, stepping back to admire me from head to toe and adjusting her cream silk scarf before she turns her dark green eyes to Edward and widens her arms again.

'My boy,' she says, hugging him to her.

'You've gotten thinner, Mum,' he says, frowning. 'You're not on one of your diets again, are you?'

Edith waves a hand at him and releases a high-pitched, thin laugh. She seems at a loss for words, which is odd for Edith, but she is saved when Jeoffrey descends the stairs and walks the long, tiled hallway towards us.

I can't help but straighten my back and I notice that Edward does the same. There's something commanding about Jeoffrey Kingston's presence.

'Sara, darling,' he says, unsmiling, and bends to press his cold lips to my cheek, giving me a whiff of his strong, piney aftershave, before he turns to Edward.

'Dad,' Edward says, offering a hand to his father. I don't believe I've ever seen the two men hug in the entire time that I've known them.

Jeoffrey regards Edward's hand but doesn't shake it, and suddenly the air in the hallway turns frosty.

Edith makes a sound in her throat and reaches beneath her scarf for the golden necklace she wears at the base of her neck – a family heirloom – her fingers stroking the tiny, acorn-shaped pendant that her mother and her grandmother and great-grandmother wore before her.

'You,' Jeoffrey says, his dark, piercing gaze resting on my husband, 'in my office.' His voice is low and ominous, like rolling thunder. 'Now.'

7

Flynn

'That bloody bitch,' says Flynn, as he raises the basket filled with golden fries out of the bubbling hot oil. 'She's doing this to get back at me,' he says, wiping sweat off his brow with the back of his other hand.

'Shouldn't we contact someone? Her family? This is the, like, seventh or eighth shift she's missed. Dani's never missed a shift. Not since I've been here,' says Sophie, tucking a lock of escaped blonde hair back into her hairnet. 'And she's not answering her phone or replying to my texts.'

'Where are those fries?' one of the girls calls out from the front counter. 'And the three cheeseburgers.'

'They're coming,' Flynn shouts back, irritated at Sophie for reasons he can't quite understand. It was all so exciting, fucking her in the cold room over the past few weeks whenever they got the chance.

He shakes salt over the hot chips as he thinks about Sophie, pants down and bent over the ice freezer. The fact that his girlfriend Dani had been working at the time and could have walked in on them at any given moment only served to heighten the pleasure. God it was good.

But now, he can't stand the sight of Sophie, and though he'll never admit it, he misses Dani. Misses her shy smile, her dark doe eyes, the softness of her long hair and the smell of her. He wishes she would text him already. It's been two bloody weeks.

'So? Should I call her family?' Sophie persists.

Flynn thinks about it while he fills the three large paper cups with hot fries, then shakes his head. No. He won't give Dani the satisfaction that he's been worrying about her.

'No. I'm sure Andrew will call them sooner or later. I'm not going to do his job for him.' He shrugs. 'And I don't give a fuck where she is, to be honest.'

He needs to pretend he doesn't care. Get Dani so desperate to see him. Then she'll come crawling back. They always do, girls like Dani. Insecure as all hell.

'What is wrong with you?' says Sophie, taking a step back and staring at him now like he has grown an extra nose. 'Gosh, you're a dick.' She storms off to the burger station to put the cheeseburgers together.

Flynn ignores Sophie and grins to himself while he watches the new girl, Lily, washing dishes at the sink. She's got a nice arse, he thinks, while he imagines her naked.

Nothing wrong with having a bit of fun while I wait for Dani to come begging, he thinks. Nothing wrong with it at all.

An hour later, while he's chatting up Lily, Sophie interrupts, her voice frosty, to tell him that there's someone out in the restaurant wanting to speak with him.

'Who is it?' he asks.

'I think it's Dani's little brother. I'm pretty sure I've seen him here before.'

Flynn puts down the tea towel that he only touched because he wanted to impress the new girl with how helpful he is, and smiles to himself.

'Dani's probably sent the little shit. I bet she's desperate to see me and wants me to come over after work.'

'She's probably sick. Of you. And she's sending her brother to tell you,' Sophie spits out.

Flynn laughs. 'As if. She's begging to take me back, one hundred percent. She can't help herself.'

Sophie rolls her eyes and walks away.

Flynn shudders as he leaves the kitchen and walks past the counter and into the restaurant. He's never realised how unattractive Sophie is until now. Funny how she seemed hot before they'd had sex, back when she was forbidden. But now, she was about as sexy as their overweight and pimply manager, Andrew.

'What's up, little bro,' Flynn says as he swaggers over to... *Harley... yeah, that's his name,* who is sitting in the booth closest to the counter, the table's surface littered with empty food containers and screwed up serviettes. *People are fucking pigs,* Flynn thinks, shaking his head.

The kid has long black hair, just brushing his shoulders. It makes him look spookily like Dani. And weirdly makes Flynn miss her even more.

Flynn hasn't had much to do with Harley while he's been dating Dani. He prefers to stay away from the families of the girls that he dates. That way there is no unnecessary beef with mums and dads and siblings when he eventually dumps the girl and runs.

'Where is she?' the boy asks, his dark eyes intense, his mouth a thin, angry line.

Flynn is momentarily struck dumb. Shouldn't this little shit know where his own sister is? A blast of anger shoots through his veins.

'Dani? How the fuck should I know? She hasn't been turning up to her shifts, the lazy bitch. I should be asking you where she is.'

The kid stiffens and stares at Flynn, his shiny black eyes unblinking.

Creepy little shit, Flynn thinks.

'So she hasn't been sleeping at your place?' the kid asks.

'No. Now you need to tell her she'd better show up to work tomorrow or she's gonna get the sack.' Flynn doesn't know this for sure, but he's hoping it'll bring Dani back.

The kid says nothing. If anything, he looks pale, like he's about to be sick.

Flynn shakes his head and turns away, but out the corner of his eye sees the kid flying out of the booth like a bat out of hell.

'Hey... what the f–'

Harley comes charging at him, knocking Flynn back against the nearby bin so hard that the metal lid comes flying off it and overflowing rubbish spills over Flynn's hair and shoulders as he slips and falls on his arse.

Customers stare at Flynn, covering their surprised mouths, a few gather around to take photos of him on their phones.

Flynn wants to tell them to fuck off, he wants to take their phones and smash them, stomp on them until they are in pieces, but he knows that Andrew, the big fat slug, will be watching via the camera on the office computer.

Harley backs away from the mess he's made, his scrawny chest rising and falling rapidly.

If Flynn wasn't in his work uniform and on shift, he'd chase the little shit and bash the living crap out of him. The kid is tall for his age but doesn't have any meat on his bones. Flynn could easily smash him.

Flynn clenches his fists as he watches Harley slip out the door and into the dark night.

Now Flynn's mad. If the kid is looking for his sister, then it means she's not sitting around home moping for

Flynn. It means Dani may have found someone else. She's probably shacked up with some loser, sleeping at his place every night. Having sex with him. Dani used to sleep at Flynn's house all the time. She'd all but moved in with him. That is, until she found out that he was fucking Sophie.

A few stragglers are still angling their phones towards him. Flynn gives them all death glares before he retreats to the greasy kitchen that he has come to hate.

8

Sara

'I'm glad the men have gone off to talk,' Edith says, pouring tea from an Alfred Meakin teapot into delicate cups and saucers.

She mentions nothing about the fact that Jeoffrey looked about ready to murder Edward before he ordered him to his office.

'Because it gives the two of us time for a nice girlie chat,' Edith says, beaming a warm smile my way.

I return her smile and brace myself for the pregnancy questions, the hints at how much she longs for grandchildren to play in the very gardens we are overlooking while we sip our tea from the back veranda.

'Oh I love this tea,' I say, after I take a sip of the strong brew. 'I'll need to get the brand off you before we head home. My mum would love it.'

'How is your mother?' Edith asks.

A willy wagtail perches on a nearby rosemary hedge and begins to chatter away at us while it flits about.

'She's okay. We chat a couple of times a week.' I smile wider when I remember that we'll be seeing her tomorrow. 'Edward and I are going to pop in and see her on our way home. It's been a while since I've seen her.'

Edith nods her head, but then quickly looks away to stare at a stunning pink rose bush. I'm not one hundred percent certain, but I think she has tears in her eyes.

'Are you okay, Edith?' I ask, sitting forward on my cushioned, wrought-iron chair.

Edith turns to face me, blinking rapidly. 'Yes, I'm fine. Just having problems with the new eyedrops my doctor prescribed me.' She lightly touches the plate of scones in front of me, and the pots of cream and homemade apricot jam. 'Please, help yourself. There's more for Edward and Jeoffrey inside.'

At the mention of the men, we both grow quiet. No doubt Edith is wondering, as am I, how the talk is going between father and son.

She must know the reason behind Jeoffrey's cold greeting and the obvious hostility he'd shown towards his only son. Surely.

'How has Edward been?' asks Edith. For the first time I notice that the lines across her forehead and around her eyes are running deeper than the last time I saw her, and she's lost a little weight.

'He's okay.' I shrug. 'A little busy at work. He really needed this getaway.'

'I bet he did,' Edith says quietly. She avoids my eyes and brushes away invisible crumbs from her pale pink blouse.

I wonder if Edith knows something that I don't. She and Edward have a special mother-son connection and I don't doubt for a moment that her intuition is picking up on the fact that something is not right with him.

'Is everything okay, Edith? I'm a little worried now. Is there something I should know?'

Edith meets my eyes and stares at me, open-mouthed as though deciding on what to say, when the back screen door squeaks and Jeoffrey steps through it and onto the veranda.

'Oh, Jeoffrey,' says Edith, seemingly both relieved and pleased with the interruption to our conversation. 'Grab a chair and join us.'

'Where's Edward?' I ask, glancing at the door.

'He's making a phone call and will be right out,' Jeoffrey says, beaming a huge smile at me, before he reaches across the table for Edith's delicate fingers and gives them a light squeeze. I could be imagining things, but I'm certain he just gave his wife a quick wink and bit of a nod.

Edith's shoulders relax and her whole face lights up, her green eyes twinkling.

'Let's have a celebratory dinner tonight,' she announces, clapping her hands together. 'We'll have champagne and I'll make Jeoffrey's favourite, roast beef.'

'What are we celebrating?' I ask, half-smiling. I'm glad that my in-laws seem more relaxed, but I can't help but wonder what's behind this sudden turnaround. Jeoffrey was so intense and cold when we first arrived. Now he's happier than I've ever seen him. Even on our wedding day he didn't smile as widely as he is right now.

Edith stares at me intently before she nods sagely, her face growing serious again.

'Life. Tonight, we will celebrate life,' she adds, her gaze no longer focused on me, but instead shifting across the garden to rest upon a budding yellow rose.

9

Sara

'Tonight was great, wasn't it?' Edward says, flopping into bed beside me and looking a lot more relaxed than when we first arrived this morning. He rolls onto his side and smiles at me, gently tugging on a lock of my dark brown hair. 'It was good to see Mum so happy.'

'It was. And they didn't say a thing when I drank all that wine and champagne at dinner.'

Edward sighs and rolls onto his back, staring up at the ceiling pensively.

'Do you think...' he says, then pauses and shakes his head. 'Actually don't worry about it.'

'What?' I ask, thinking now is the perfect time to probe my husband for more information. Alcohol has always made Edward extra chatty. 'You can tell me anything, you know.'

'I know,' he says, his voice soft. He closes his eyes and I realise, after all the wine and bubbly he's consumed, that if I'm not careful he'll fall asleep.

'Hey Eddie,' I say, snuggling up to him. 'What did your father want to talk to you about?'

Edward stiffens beside me for a moment, and then exhales softly. 'Oh, the usual. Wanting me to take over the family business now that he's retiring. I think eventually he'd like us to move here and live with them.'

'Your dad said that? Really?' I ask.

Jeoffrey has always struck me as a man who guards his privacy. Whenever we come to stay, although he's always happy to see us, he is usually his most relaxed on the morning that we leave.

Edward doesn't answer me, and when I raise my head to check, I can see that his eyes are closed, and his breathing has grown heavy.

I poke his shoulder, but he doesn't flinch. If anything, he begins to snore softly.

Sighing, I roll over and contemplate staying up to read the new book I purchased especially for this trip but decide to get an early night instead. But before I can even think about sleep, I'll need a glass of water and some paracetamol for the champagne headache I can feel coming on.

Careful not to wake my husband, I ease my way out of bed and step out into the hallway, the tiles cool beneath my feet as I make my way to the kitchen.

The house is dark. I slide my hand along the smooth, cream-coloured walls until my fingers find the switch and the kitchen is illuminated by the many LED lights embedded in the ceiling.

I squint beneath the harsh glare until my eyes adjust.

The marble countertops gleam beneath the lights and the stainless-steel sink sparkles. Edith is a stickler for cleanliness. I need to take a leaf out of her book. Though I keep our lovely home decently tidy, I don't really take the time to make it shine like this. It's impressive. Especially considering she has always had the means to pay for a cleaner, but never has, despite how huge the house is.

Once I've found the paracetamol and water, I decide to make a cup of camomile tea to take to bed with me. While I'm waiting for the kettle to boil, I head to the nearby guest bathroom to go to the toilet.

I'm surprised by the strip of light at the base of the door. Perhaps one of my in-laws left it on by mistake.

I lightly rap on the door with my knuckles but get no response.

'Hello? Is someone in there?'

Again, no response.

I twist the door handle. It's not locked so I open the door, only to feel someone push it shut from the other side.

'Get out!' Edith shouts, her voice steely. I've never heard her sound so angry before.

My pulse thunders in my ears as I stand there in my silk pyjamas, shocked, my arms covered in goosebumps.

'Are you okay?' I ask, keeping my voice calm, hoping she'll respond in turn.

'Go away, Sara,' she hisses. 'Just please, go away.'

10

Neve

'We need to talk,' says Stan.

It's Sunday morning, and while Jake is at a sleepover, Stan has driven me out to a lovely spot for breakfast. It's a cute little café which extends to a garden nursery where he likes to buy his rose bushes from.

'Okay,' I say, pushing my plate of unfinished poached eggs aside. I want to take another sip of my coffee, but I know that by now it has grown cold.

'What's happened to us, Neve?' he says, his eyes reddening with emotion. 'We used to be such a–'

'I know,' I say.

'But what's different?' he asks. 'How did you go from a woman wanting to...' – he glances around to make sure that nobody is listening before continuing, his cheeks blushing pink – 'to someone who–'

'How was breakfast?' asks a young waitress, interrupting Stan's conversation, which is way too heavy for the pretty, garden setting, and the company we're in. The tables around us are all filled with couples or young families, enjoying their weekend together.

'Wonderful,' I say, smiling wide, despite my unfinished plate. I'm so grateful for her interruption.

'Neve, I'm not finished. There are questions I need answered,' he says after the waitress leaves with our plates, his lips a thin line.

I glance over my shoulder and smile at the elderly couple sitting behind us before turning back to Stan.

'There are questions I need answered too. Like where on earth is my daughter? Why did she leave so suddenly? And why is she only speaking to you? And when in the hell is your brother going to leave?'

Stan looks at me for a long time, before he opens his mouth to speak.

'I'm going to pay the bill,' he says, and scrapes his metal chair back so loudly a child seated at the table beside us covers his ears with his hands and squeezes his eyes shut.

11

Sara

'I'm worried about your mum,' I say to Edward, as I watch the greenery whizzing past us through the passenger window.

Whenever we leave Jeoffrey and Edith's place, I always find myself feeling a little melancholy, mourning the loss of the fresh country air and nature ahead of time. So I'm making a point to keep my head up and to focus on the scenery we're leaving behind, so that I can mentally take it back with me to the suburbs.

Edward's knuckles tighten around the steering wheel. 'Why do you say that? Did she say something?'

I tell him about last night, how I tried to enter the bathroom and how Edith yelled at me to get out and shoved the door closed.

Edward shrugs. 'Mum and Dad's en-suite shower is on the blink. She was probably using the main bathroom and you interrupted her. That doesn't sound too weird.'

'Oh, okay,' I say, relaxing against my leather seat. 'That makes sense.' But then I recall the way she'd sounded, the desperation in her voice. 'She just sounded scared... and maybe angry too. I'm not sure how to explain it. And when I went to find your dad, he was in his study texting someone. He jumped when he saw me standing in the doorway. Like he'd been sprung doing something that he shouldn't be doing.'

Edward takes one hand off the wheel and reaches for my hand. He gives my fingers a gentle squeeze.

'You're such an overthinker, Sars. I'm glad you care so much for my mum. But I'm sure she's okay. And as for my dad, he's allowed to text people, you know. Just because he's older than us doesn't mean he can't have a life.' Edward laughs. 'Everything is okay, Sars, please don't worry.'

'I hope so,' I say. But although I admit that I overthink at times, I do trust my instincts, and they are telling me that something isn't right with Edith and Jeoffrey.

I sigh and again focus my attention on the sheep-dotted pastures and the cloudy sky through the passenger window. Take a chill pill, is what Edward is trying to say. And maybe he's right.

For the remainder of the trip, I try not to obsess over anything and instead focus on the fact that Edward did not once, for the entire stay, mention any talk of us having a baby, and neither did his parents. Perhaps everyone has finally gotten the message that I won't be carrying a child ever again.

I sneak a glance at Edward and note how relaxed he seems. He looks good too, as though somehow, magically, this weekend has reversed the aging process by about five years.

He seems a lot happier, and even whistled a tune while we loaded the boot of the car before we left. And then he hugged both his parents, which is something he never does. Usually it's a quick peck on the cheek for his mum and a handshake with his dad.

Jeoffrey seemed extra jovial too. As though that tense moment when we arrived had never happened.

A sigh of contentment escapes my lips as I recline against the seat.

My husband was right. We needed this weekend away. And now I'm so glad that I agreed to it.

By the time we pull into one of the guest carparks at my mother's apartment complex, I'm feeling recharged, and excited to see my mum. I can't wait to give her the bag of goodies we've put together for her, including some handmade chocolates we purchased at a quaint little boutique store along the way, and a box of Edith's favourite tea leaves.

But when I knock on her apartment door, there's no answer, which is strange seeing as she's expecting us and seemed genuinely looking forward to seeing me when I called her to tell her the news.

'Mum?' I call out as I knock again.

'Did you hear that?' asks Edward, pressing his ear to the door. 'Sounded like a thump. Someone's in there.'

I nudge Edward aside and knock again.

'Mum, open up please.' I rest my ear against the door while I try to listen. The white door still smells like fresh paint. The complex was brand new when Mum moved in last year.

The door springs open and I nearly fall into the apartment, but don't, thanks to Edward grabbing a hold of me.

But it's not my mother standing there. Instead, Bill, my mother's old boyfriend grins at me, showing me how yellow his teeth have gotten. He's the bright spark who smashed up her last apartment and lost my mother her $800 bond and got her kicked out.

I wrinkle my nose and take a step back. Bill reeks of bad odour and stale beer. How my mother can stand to be around him is beyond me.

'Where's my mum?'

'In the shower. She had a big night. Can't handle her drink,' he says, with a sniff.

'We'll wait inside for her,' I say. 'You can leave if you like, Bill.'

Bill draws his head back and raises his eyebrows. 'I'm not leaving my own home for anybody.'

My blood immediately boils. Edward puts a hand to my lower back, as though to remind me to keep calm, but I can't help it.

'Your home? This is my mother's apartment. We make the payments so that she can live here, not you. So you can leave right now, thank you.'

Bill laughs, and we're treated to a waft of garlic and stale beer breath.

'I'm not going anywhere. And you can't come in. Carmella and I have plans.'

'Mum,' I call out, trying to push past Bill, but he remains rooted to the spot.

'Sara,' Mum calls from behind Bill.

Bill steps aside and laughs at the surprised look on my face.

'What, did you think I'd murdered her?' he says, before he disappears into the darkness of the apartment.

Mum comes to the door, wearing an old purple robe I'd bought her for Mother's Day when I was in my teens, just before I left home. It was around the time Mum started getting boyfriends like Bill. When I decided that it was easier to leave home and live on the streets than it was to remain there and watch my mother allow her boyfriends to treat her like rubbish and spend what little money she had on beers and smokes.

Though the dressing gown has frayed edges and has faded with age, Mum once told me that she'll never get a new one because this one meant so much to her and soothed her aching heart for many a year while she missed me after I'd left home.

'Hi Mum, can we come in?'

Mum glances over her shoulder, steps out of the apartment and pulls the door almost shut, leaving it slightly ajar.

'Bill's having a bit of a tough time so I'm just helping him out. Sorry. He showed up on Friday night out of the blue.'

She looks so tired, with dark circles beneath her eyes.

'Mum, he told us he lives here.'

'Quiet, or he'll hear you,' she hisses, frowning. 'He's just staying for the time being, until he finds his feet.'

'You mean until you run out of money.'

Mum puts her hands to her face and smooths her fringe out of her eyes. She has always had such pretty, sparkling blue eyes. No matter how old she gets, Mum's stunning eyes never fail to twinkle with a youthfulness that betrays all the wrinkles she earnt from a lifetime of hard living.

'I know what I'm doing, Sara.'

'No you don't, Mum.'

We stare each other down for around half a minute before Edward places a hand on my shoulder and gives me a squeeze.

'Would you like to come out for a drive with us, Carmella? We could go out for coffee. You and Sara can have a proper catch-up.' He holds up the gift bag loaded with treats for her. 'This is for you, by the way.'

Mum smiles at Edward. 'Thank you, love. That's very kind of you.' She lightly touches his cheek and takes the bag. 'You're a sweetheart, Eddie,' she says, before she rests her gaze on me. 'Both of you are so wonderful. But I'm going to have to say no to the coffee because I've got last-minute plans.'

Her eyes glaze over with tears, but she blinks them away.

'Just for ten minutes, Mum,' I say. 'A quick one.'

'Sorry, love.' A look of annoyance flashes across Mum's face before she reaches out and takes my hand in hers. 'It's been so good to see you. Thank you so much for coming around and checking on me.' She lets me go. 'But I'm okay, as you can see.'

'I don't think you are,' I say, softly.

Mum places a trembling hand over her throat, masking the deep wrinkles there, then tucks her greying hair behind her ear. 'How about we do this next weekend instead? Please? I really do want to spend some quality time with you. With you both,' she adds, smiling at Edward.

'That sounds like a great idea,' says my husband.

I'd be lying if I said I wasn't disappointed that I'm not going to be spending the afternoon with Mum. But I suppose it is what it is.

'Okay. But promise me Bill will be gone by then. You know he's bad news. You've worked so hard to get your life back on track, Mum, don't throw it away for some creep who treats you like an ATM machine.'

'I can hear you,' he calls from somewhere deep in the apartment. 'And it's hurting my feelings.'

'Good,' I shout back.

'I'd better go,' Mum says. She gives me and Edward a quick hug each before disappearing into her apartment, leaving behind the scent of her favourite perfume.

'Call or text me anytime,' I say, even though the door is now shut. 'I'll come at midnight if you need me. Anytime. I'm here for you,' I say, pressing my palm flat against the door.

No response.

I sigh and Edward gently takes my hand away from the door and draws me to his side. We walk like this all the way to the car, Edward with an arm around my shoulders, and me leaning into him, my arms circled around his waist.

'Thank you,' I say, once we're back on the road heading for home.

'For what?' asks Edward.

'For being so supportive, you know, with my situation with Mum.'

'It is what it is,' he says. 'She's a grown woman. I know you're disappointed with how today turned out, but you've got to let her make her own choices... and mistakes.'

'Yeah, I know. It's hard not to worry though,' I say. It's hard not to feel guilty as well, but I don't say that out loud.

Though I was only a teenager when I left home, I still feel as though I let my mother down somehow by leaving her. Maybe that's why I feel compelled to watch over her now, and to make sure that she knows I'm always here for her.

My husband gives my hand a squeeze, as though reading my thoughts, then lets me go to turn on the radio.

The news is on, and Edward and I share a look of dread.

> *The body found in the Lakeland Gardens waters has been identified as twenty-year-old Hilton resident, Danielle Stokes. Police are asking those with any information to please contact their local stations or call 1300 5555.*

Edward sighs deeply. I can read his mind.

He's glad that it's not Liv and feels guilty for feeling relieved about it when someone out there has lost their precious daughter. I know this because I feel the same way.

We pull into our local petrol station to refuel, and I notice that Harley is absent today. He always washes windows at the lights on Sundays.

After Edward has filled the tank, he reaches in through the window for his wallet.

'We need milk and bread too, please,' I say. 'Get the sandwich loaf, not the toast this time.'

'Hey,' he says, making a face. 'They should label those things better.'

As I watch Edward disappear inside the store, my phone pings with a text.

It's from Neve.

> *Meet me tomorrow evening at the Beach Bar Café 7pm. I need to talk to you about something important. Come alone.*

12

Sara

Because it's a Monday night, the popular café and restaurant strip is a little quieter than usual and I easily snag a parking bay right out in front of the Beach Bar Café.

I can't see Neve's car, but sometimes she gets Stan to drop her off if she plans on drinking a lot. I hope tonight isn't one of those nights because I'm still exhausted after the weekend and need an early night.

Last night I didn't get much sleep because my head was filled with worries about Mum. And when I did manage to finally drift off in the early hours of the morning, my dreams were tainted with Bill and his menacing stare and cigarette-stained teeth.

But if Neve needs me, I can suffer a few more hours before I rest my head on my pillow tonight. The least I can do for my best friend is to listen to whatever she needs to get off her chest and then get her home safely.

As soon as I enter the restaurant, my stomach grumbles at the delicious aroma of seafood and garlic wafting from the kitchen.

Waitstaff chat by the bar between taking table orders. Music plays in the background, something hip and alternative – the kind of music you imagine surfers would listen to, just loud enough to be heard over the customers' conversations. The restaurant isn't exactly packed with customers, but it's not empty either.

I head straight out the back to the outdoor seating area, where I know Neve will be waiting for me.

As soon as I step outside, the salty ocean breeze caresses my face and sweeps my hair back over my shoulders. I can never get enough of the ocean. Just like the countryside, the vastness of the ocean never fails to remind me of how small we are and of how big the world is. It helps to put everything into perspective and to remind me that in the grand scheme of things, we are but tiny dots in the universe and our problems even tinier.

My stomach twists when I spot her, sitting with her back to me at the far end table to my left, her long, pale blonde hair wrapped up in a low bun. She's wearing a white jacket with the collars turned up to protect her from the cool sea breeze, which makes her look like a diminutive ice queen.

I'm wearing blue, which suits my olive skin and dark hair. Neve always says that our differences complement each other's beauty perfectly.

The ocean looks dark and endless, both dangerous and beautiful under the moonlight. It makes Neve look so tiny and alone sitting in front of it, a near-empty bottle of prosecco and a crystal flute to keep her company.

She doesn't turn to the sound of my heels clacking against the polished jarrah decking, instead she continues staring out at the glittering, black sea.

'Neve,' I say, ever so softly, placing a gentle hand on her shoulder.

She bristles and then exhales when she sees that it's me.

'Sorry, I was away with the fairies,' she says, blinking up at me and then back at the sea.

I bend down to give her a hug, catching a whiff of the gardenia and jasmine perfume she loves, and then join her at the table, choosing the chair beside her so that we can watch the ocean together. Sometimes it's easier to talk when you're sitting side by side rather than face to face. I'm hoping it helps her to get whatever it is that she needs off her chest.

'Are you okay, Neve?'

'Wait,' Neve says and signals for a young, stylishly dressed waiter to bring another bottle of prosecco and an additional flute.

'Only one drink for me,' I say. 'I'm driving.'

Neve sighs with disappointment and her cute button nose crinkles.

'Get Eddie to pick you up later. Or get a lift home with me when Stan picks me up later. You can leave your car here.'

'On any other night I'd say yes, but not tonight.' I cover my mouth and yawn before relaxing against the back of my chair.

'Tired?' she asks.

'Yeah. We visited Jeoffrey and Edith over the weekend.' I decide not to mention my mum and the fact that she ditched me for Bill yesterday afternoon. Because if I do, I might embarrassingly blubber up like a five-year-old. And tonight isn't about me, it's about Neve.

'Oh, okay,' Neve says, her voice so tiny and mouselike.

My head throbs faintly with the headache that hasn't really left since Saturday night at Edward's parents' place.

'Thank you,' we both say in unison as the waiter places a fresh bottle on the table, along with a bucket of ice, then hands me a clean flute.

I pour the drinks and pass Neve hers. Despite the bottle she's already consumed, she doesn't seem as intoxicated as I'd expect her to be.

She casts her blue-eyed gaze out across the sea.

'Liv loves this beach so much. I honestly cannot believe she swapped this for Melbourne when it's always so cold over there.'

'Yeah, it is kind of weird,' I say. 'But it is a gorgeous city.'

'Yeah. True,' says Neve, shrugging.

'How is she?' I ask.

Neve is quiet for a long moment.

'I wouldn't know. She only talks to Stan.'

'Oh,' I say. 'I was hoping you'd have spoken to her by now.'

'You and me both.'

The fact that Liv messages Stan only is strange. Neve and Liv have always been close, they have the kind of relationship most mothers dream of having with their daughters. Sure, they have their arguments like most parents and their kids do, but they've always been close.

'Have you tried reaching out to her again?' I ask, but as soon as the words leave my lips, I wish I could take them back.

Neve's chin wobbles a little and her eyes fill with tears.

'Yes. I have. She never responds.'

'Oh, I'm so sorry.'

Neve blinks several times, her eyes deep in thought.

'For some reason Stan is in the good books and I'm in the bad,' she says, frowning.

I'm not sure what to say to this, because I have no answers and find it just as puzzling as Neve does.

A long silence descends between us as we both watch a flock of seagulls circling the silvery, moonlit shore.

'You know, Stan and I haven't had sex in over two years,' Neve blurts out. 'I don't think he finds me attractive anymore.'

I'm quiet for a few seconds. While I knew that Neve and Stan had been having issues in the bedroom, I didn't realise that things were this bad. I thought that maybe they were having less sex, not no sex at all.

'I'm sure that's not true, Neve. What makes you think that he's not attracted to you anymore?'

Neve takes a sip of her drink. 'I just have a feeling. He seems to need a different kind of sex to get him off. So I guess plain old me is not... enough.'

I'm quiet for at least half a minute and take a couple of long gulps of my prosecco, the bubbles almost painfully fizzing against the roof of my mouth. Because I'm not sure how to react to this bombshell.

'I'm so sorry.' I say, when I finally speak. 'That must be tough.'

'Don't be. To be honest, it's me that doesn't want it anymore. The sex. Something happened after I did all that damage when giving birth to Jake.' Neve shudders. 'And as the years pass, I've just... something's come over me. I don't want Stan near me anymore. His touch... it repulses me. I don't even have fantasies about that footy player anymore. You know, the one with the mullet? It's as though I'm just... blank down there.'

I swipe my finger through the condensation on my flute, leaving a shiny streak against the glass.

'Fair enough,' I say. Edward hates when I use 'fair enough' in conversation. He thinks it's a cop-out from saying what I really think. But in this case, I'm not thinking anything. I just want to be a listener. A soft place for Neve to fall.

'Have you talked to Stan about it all? What does he

think?' I ask.

'Since Lawrence has come to stay our communication has gone down the toilet.' She sighs. 'I found a pair of my underwear in the pocket of Lawrence's pants when I was doing his laundry. But when I questioned Stan about it, he got all sensitive and yelled at me to mind my own business. He argued that other women might have the same underwear as me and said that his brother is allowed to have sexual relationships. Which is true. But Stan's reaction was so intense... it was weird. And I am one hundred percent sure that it was my underwear.'

I shudder at the idea of Lawrence going through Neve's underwear drawer.

'That's so creepy, Neve. Maybe Lawrence staying over is stressing out Stan more than he's letting on?'

'I don't know. I don't know what my husband is thinking anymore.'

'Stan thinks this conversation is over,' says a low, gravelly voice from behind us.

Neve gasps, and I sit up straight, open-mouthed and in shock, as Stan comes to stand on the opposite side of the table, blocking our stunning view of the Indian Ocean. He rests his hands on the edge of the wooden table, tilting it slightly.

'Stan,' I say, plastering a warm smile on my face, my heart beating in my throat. 'I didn't know you'd be joining us. I'd have asked Eddie if I knew.'

Stan doesn't meet my eyes. Instead he opens his wallet and takes out several one-hundred-dollar notes and leaves them on the table beneath the ice bucket. Way too much for two bottles of prosecco.

'We haven't even ordered our food,' says Neve. She flicks at the edges of the money poking out. 'And I don't need your money, I can pay for this myself.'

He glares at Neve, then at me, and rakes a hand through his hair. He looks angry and his eyes look frighteningly wild, as though he's trying his hardest not to lash out at us in front of the few occupied tables to the right.

'Stan, we were just...' I fumble to find the right words. 'We're discussing women's issues... girl talk. That's all this is. Neve needs a chat. And so do I.' I try smiling again. 'Come on, let us girls do our thing, just like you and Eddie do sometimes. I'll drop Neve home at a respectable hour.' I gesture to my glass, which has a few mouthfuls left in it. 'This is the only drink I plan on having tonight. So I'll be good to drive.'

Stan curls his lips and speaks through clenched teeth.

'I heard my name, Sara,' he says, his voice ice cold. 'I'm not stupid. And to be frank, this is the last thing I need – Neve off her tree while she's on her meds and coming out in public sharing our private business. Our family is going through a lot right now, with Liv being gone. The least you could do is respect our fucking privacy.'

Stan's speech shocks me into silence. Up until recently, I've never seen this side of my husband's best friend, and I'm starkly reminded of the fact that we never truly know anyone, not our friends, not our parents, and certainly not our partners.

'We're leaving,' he says to Neve, his pale blue eyes frosty.

Neve stares up at him, her eyes wide. She looks frightened of her own husband. 'But I'm not on any meds...'

'There you go again, Neve. Lying and making up stories. Let's get you home to rest.'

'Wait a minute,' I say, standing up, feeling protective of my tiny friend. 'We were having a private conversation. You can't just barge in on us and demand Neve leaves. She has her own mind.'

Stan's face flushes pink. People are starting to stare.

A young waiter hovers nearby, clutching a neat pile of cloth napkins, perhaps unsure whether to intervene or not.

'You stay out of this, Sara. This is between me and my wife,' he hisses.

Neve stares up at the both of us, speechless. Her head wobbles a little, as though the alcohol has finally caught up with her.

'Neve, I can take you home in a bit if you still want to talk,' I say, ignoring Stan's reddening face and his sighs of impatience.

'No. She's coming home with me. Now. Up,' he says, speaking to her like she is a dog.

Neve stands and sways on her feet, clutching at the back of the chair.

Stan grabs a hold of her arm and guides her away from the table and to his side.

'Sorry, Sara. Let's do this again... some other time,' she says, her eyes shiny and her gaze far away, staring into space.

'Are you sure you're ready to leave?' I ask, not liking the way Stan's fingers are digging into Neve's arm.

She blinks and her eyes gain focus, then she nods. 'I'm tired now. Bye, Sara.'

Stan glares at me over his shoulder, several times, as he leads Neve back through the restaurant and out the front entrance and onto the street.

Most of the people sitting nearby turn back to their plates of seafood and their conversations now that Neve and Stan are gone. I decide to sit back down and finish my glass of prosecco and try my best to enjoy the view. It gives me a chance to try and dissect what just happened.

But no matter how many minutes pass, or how many sips of bubbly I take, the situation doesn't become any clearer. The plain truth is that Stan acted creepy and stalker-like with Neve, showing up like that and listening in on our private conversation. He is being a control freak. I can't believe he showed up like that and took her home as though she has no will of her own. And he was so rough with her.

I drain the last of my drink and when I put down my flute, I spy a dark-haired, teenage boy wandering around the inside part of the restaurant, moving from table to table, his dark eyes trained on all the men's faces, as though he's looking for someone.

As soon as he steps outside, I rise to my feet.

'Harley?' I call out, not believing my eyes.

The boy turns to face me and his eyes light up with recognition.

'What on earth are you doing in here?' I ask.

He approaches my table without the smile he normally greets me with when I'm in my car at the traffic lights.

'I'm looking for someone,' he says, his dark eyes fixed on Neve's lipstick-smeared flute.

Harley looks so much younger in this place, the sharp lines of his teenage jaw and cheekbones softened in the dim glow of the fairy lights strung above us.

'Oh. Can I help in any way?' I ask.

He looks at me, his eyes loaded with questions, or maybe answers, and then he looks away and mutters something that sounds like, *yeah, you can tell me where he is.*

13

Sara

'What was that?' I ask, over the sounds of the ocean rushing to the shore, the murmuring conversations all around us, and the music drifting out from inside of the restaurant.

'Don't worry. Nothing. I could be wrong.' Harley stares at me for a long time, his chest rising and falling with pent-up emotion. 'He's not here. I'll keep looking.'

'Wait,' I say, when he turns away.

After hesitating for a few seconds, he turns back around.

'In case you need it.' I take a twenty-dollar note out of my purse and offer it to him. 'I didn't see you on Sunday.'

Harley takes the money and pockets it in his jeans, avoiding my eyes.

'Why weren't you there, Harley? Is everything okay with you? With your family?'

Harley blinks and I'm shocked to see several tears spill over his cheeks.

'Oh, no. What's wrong?'

I move to get closer, but I accidentally kick the leg of my chair.

The sound startles him, he backs away, and like a frightened nocturnal creature he runs back through the restaurant, narrowly missing a waitress balancing two large steaming bowls of chilli mussels in each hand, and disappears out onto the street.

Goosebumps dot my arms and I rub at them, while I stand there and try my best to understand what had just happened.

A little while later, when I arrive home, I'm still thinking about Harley, wondering who he was looking for and why. And what he meant when he said, 'Yeah, you can tell me where he is.' Who did he mean? And why would I know where this person is?

Harley has never told me much about himself. Just that he has two older sisters, that his father is no longer employed because of an old work injury, and that his mother does ironing for the women in the more affluent suburbs to make ends meet. But seeing as our conversations are had in the thirty seconds it takes for him to wash my car windscreen, those titbits about his family are quite generous. I just wish that he'd talk about himself a little more. He seems so troubled of late.

The house is dark when I get home. Edward isn't in yet. He texted earlier, before I met up with Neve, to say he won't be back until around 10pm because work 'is crazy', so I take a shower and get into my pyjamas, then make myself a cup of tea and some toast, taking it all into the living room.

As soon as I turn the television on and set my mug and plate on the coffee table, somebody knocks on my front door.

I check my phone. It's only 8.30pm, but for a Monday night, it is most definitely not the norm to have someone banging on our door at this time.

'Who is it?' I call out from the hallway, before I tiptoe back into the living room and take a quick peek through the curtains.

Stan's black Porsche SUV gleams in our driveway beneath the streetlight.

Great. He's the last person I want to see right now.

Maybe he feels awful for how he behaved at the Beach Bar Café.

I cast my steaming mug of tea and jam toast a long look before I sigh and open the front door, leaving the screen door locked.

'It's you,' I say, taking a step back and folding my arms across my chest.

'I know, I know,' says Stan, offering his palms up. 'I've been an arsehole. I feel awful. I'm so sorry, Sara,' he says, giving me puppy dog eyes. 'Please forgive me?'

This is more like the Stan I know. Soft, gentle, kind Stan.

I sigh and unlock the screen door. 'Of course I forgive you. But I hope you've apologised to Neve. She's the one you should be talking to right now, not me.'

'I've already apologised to Neve,' he says, sighing deeply.

Stan steps inside and closes the door behind him.

We sit on opposite couches in the living room and the air between us is stiff and awkward without Edward and Neve accompanying us.

'Would you like a tea or coffee? Wine?'

He shakes his head and stands, pacing the living room carpet.

'No, thanks. I just want to help you understand what's been happening with Neve.'

'Oh okay,' I say.

Stan stops pacing and looks me dead in the eye.

'This is going to sound crazy, but... I think Neve is having an affair.'

It takes me a long time to reply. Because what he is suggesting is downright ridiculous.

'An affair?' After what Neve just told me about not wanting sex with her own husband since having Jake, and feeling as though she's 'blank' downstairs, I can hardly believe she'd go around screwing another man.

'No way. That *is* crazy. What makes you think that?'

Stan rakes a trembling hand through his hair. He is clearly rattled.

'You know,' he says, swallowing down a harsh laugh. 'In the beginning I thought it was Eddie.'

'Edward?' I frown in confusion. 'Honestly, Stan, what are you on? Edward would never do that to you, or to me.'

'He's been acting off. Funny. I don't know how to explain it. Secretive I guess.'

Reluctantly I nod. Okay. I can agree with that at least. Edward has been secretive and a bit strange lately.

My stomach starts to churn, and I realise that I've only got a glass of prosecco and a single sip of sweet tea in there.

'You know on Friday, when you both showed up, and then Edward and I were in the kitchen before he stormed out the house and drove off?'

'Yes,' I say quickly, impatient to know what Stan is about to tell me.

'It's because I accused him of sleeping with Neve.'

'What?' My heart hammers against my chest in alarm. 'How could you accuse Eddie of that? He's your best friend.'

'Well I did. Anyway, he had a go at me, tried to punch me after I said it. That's why my button was missing. He'd grabbed me by the collar.'

I say nothing as my blood runs cold. This is a completely different story to what my husband told me.

'Did he tell you that?' Stan asks.

I shake my head, unable to speak.

Stan nods knowingly and resumes pacing.

'I'm worried about Eddie, Sara,' he says. 'Really fucking concerned for my best mate.'

'So am I,' I say, my words barely a whisper. 'But I know that he would never... well I don't know, do I? But not Neve. No. No way.'

'But you've noticed the incessant beeping of his

phone, and the way he disappears without warning or explanation?' He shakes his head and stabs at the air with a finger. 'If it's not my wife he's seeing, then it's someone else.'

There's a gleam in Stan's eyes that I don't like. It's almost like he's taking great pleasure in bringing down my husband, his best friend. When we first met, Edward filled me in about Stan's almost obsessive competitiveness against Edward, which dates all the way back to their high-school years.

'I think you should leave, Stan,' I say, my voice tight.

He stops pacing and looks at me, his brows raised in surprise.

'I get it,' he says. 'It's hard to hear. You need time to digest this.'

'Maybe,' I manage to say, as I walk to the front door and hold it open for him.

'If you need anything,' he says, from the doorstep, 'call me. You and Eddie are family to us.'

I nod, resisting the urge to slam the door in his face.

'Oh, Neve is okay, by the way,' he says, as though attempting to keep the conversation between us alive, when all I want to do is put it to rest. Edward and Neve? How dare Stan even suggest it?

'Is she upset?' I ask, as the screen door closes with a click.

'No. She's sleeping it off.' He shrugs. 'She shouldn't even be drinking when she's on her meds. They make her... not right. Neve told me mixing the two makes her do strange things. She lies sometimes. But she can't help it. It's not her fault,' he says, his eyes red with unshed tears.

A cool breeze blows in through the screen door and I shiver and fold my arms across my chest.

'Neve hasn't mentioned that she's taking any meds,' I say, puzzled. Neve usually tells me everything.

'Yeah. Antidepressants. She started them a month or

so ago.'

'Oh,' is all I can say. 'Well, I'll make sure to give her a call in the morning. Check up on her.'

Stan nods and walks away, but then turns back, his hands fidgeting inside his trouser pockets. His skin looks silvery in the moonlight.

'Actually, it would be great if you left Neve alone for a bit. The doctor said it's best for her to not be stressed while her body is adjusting to her new meds.'

'I'm her best friend, Stan. I'm not going to stress her out.' I look at him and shake my head, annoyed that he thinks he has the right to gatekeep his wife. 'And no offense, but maybe having your brother come to stay isn't exactly the most relaxing experience for Neve. Have you thought about that?'

'What did she tell you about Lawrence?'

'What Neve and I speak about is our business. You need to go home and talk to her. Listen to what she has to say.'

Stan sighs and takes a step towards the screen door.

'Okay. Maybe you're right. But I think you need to back off and give us some space too, okay?' He steps closer then lowers his voice after the next-door neighbour's porch light comes on. 'I think you need to be focusing on your own marriage, not mine, Sara.'

'Fair enough,' I say, after a long pause, but only so that I can get rid of him.

He's an idiot if he thinks I'm going to listen to him. Of course I'll be contacting Neve in the morning to check up on her. She's my best friend and Stan doesn't get to dictate whether I speak to her or not.

After I watch Stan drive away, I text Edward to tell him that Stan's been around and that I've got a lot to speak to him about when he gets home.

But the message sits undelivered.

I sip my now cold tea and grimace at the bitter taste in my mouth. Then I take a bite of the cold toast and then another, until both slices are gone.

Edward has been behaving strangely lately. I'll give Stan that.

But Stan has been acting weird, too.

Someone isn't telling me the truth about that day in the kitchen at Stan and Neve's.

And I'm going to do my best to find out who and why.

14

Neve

Stan thinks I'm asleep, but he's delusional if he believes that I can relax enough to sleep with the million and one thoughts terrorising my brain.

He tiptoed into the room only minutes ago, after he returned from wherever it is that he disappeared to for half an hour – I heard his car – and started snoring almost immediately. As though he doesn't have a care in the world. And maybe he doesn't. Maybe because Liv is keeping him in the loop he can sleep like a baby, content in knowing that he has a daughter who loves and trusts him.

Thinking about Liv is so painful. If my heart were made of glass, I'd have tiny fractures all over it for every time my daughter enters my thoughts. If I think about her anymore, I'm certain my heart is going to shatter into pieces.

No matter how many hours I lie awake at night,

wondering what led to Liv running off to Melbourne so suddenly, without saying goodbye to me, I simply cannot figure it out. It's so out of character for my daughter to not include me in something so huge.

She didn't even say goodbye to my mother, and she loves her nana. She's always been so close to Sara and Edward, too. They're her godparents. For her to have shut them out as well has me so worried.

Stan grunts and rolls over, flopping an arm over my chest. His hand moves around, groping for my right breast, and when he finds it, he gives it a squeeze.

I want to scratch his eyes out – I'm still mad at him for showing up at the Beach Bar Café like that and spoiling my private chat with Sara – but instead I make fake snuffling noises, sleep sounds, as I roll over and face the window. Thank God Stan's hand slides down my back like a dead slug and flops onto the mattress.

It's a shame that I didn't get to continue my conversation with Sara. Because I was hoping that we could have eventually discussed the situation with Liv some more after I'd offloaded all the relationship issues Stan and I are going through. I've never been one to discuss relationship issues with my friends – even Sara, whom I'm super close with. But the past year I've started opening up to her, because it's gotten to the point that I need to tell someone before I implode.

I sigh and stare out the bedroom window, where I can see a patch of inky sky.

Where are you, Liv? Are you staring at the same sky right now? I love you so much. Why did you leave? What made you so upset that you couldn't say goodbye to me?

The only thing that comes to mind is the thing I did with Stan.

The thing that never fails to make me sick whenever I think of it.

What kind of a woman am I to have done such a thing?

That night, in the living room, after way too much wine… it was a mistake.

A mistake that I'm sure will haunt me forever.

My biggest regret.

But surely Liv doesn't know about that.

Nobody knows.

Except for Stan and me.

15

Sara

I'm in bed, half-asleep when Edward finally returns home. Through blurry, sleepy eyes, I check my phone on my bedside table. It's 12am.

'Where have you been? It's the middle of the night. You said you'd be home at ten,' I say, unable to keep the accusation out of my croaky voice. Stan's impromptu visit, and the questions he planted inside my mind, has left me not only irritated, but paranoid too.

Now I feel foolish for thinking, while driving through the countryside with Edward yesterday, that we had grown so much closer as a couple over the course of the weekend.

Edward puts a finger to his lips and makes a shushing sound. He wobbles on his feet as he tries to kick off his shoes.

'Are you drunk?' I ask, sitting up, wide awake now.

He runs his fingers through his hair and blinks, then shakes his head. 'No. I only had… four, no, five drinks… I think.'

'Well I'm trying to sleep,' I say, rolling over to face the bedroom window so that I don't have to look at my intoxicated husband.

Edward laughs, like a hyena.

I stuff my head deeper into my pillow.

'You don't need sleep, Sars. It's not like you have to go to work tomorrow,' he says.

'No thanks to you,' I mutter.

'What's that supposed to mean?'

He slides into bed, bringing with him the pungent smell of stale bourbon on his breath.

Cold fingers slide over my bare shoulder, and I flinch in response.

'I said, what's that supposed to mean?'

'I don't want to get into it,' I say, pulling the doona up and over my shoulder so that he can't touch me. 'We can talk about it in the morning.'

Edward strokes my hair and then he presses his cold, wet lips to my neck and I shudder. Sex is the last thing on my mind tonight.

'Not tonight, Edward,' I say, thinking about Neve and what she confessed to me earlier, and then the things Stan told me afterwards. 'I've had a real shitty night. If you'd taken the time to read my message, you would have come home instead of staying out drinking.'

'Well... I'm... I kind of... I've been busy.'

He continues to press his wet lips against my neck and then his hands find my hips beneath the bedcovers and in a single, aggressive move, very unlike the usually gentle-handed Edward, he tugs my pyjama pants down my hips.

'Hey, stop,' I say, desperately trying to pull my pyjamas up as I squirm away from my husband, who has now pressed himself against me. 'Get away from me.'

His fingers dig into my hips.

'Just once more... without protection,' he says, slurring his words. 'We might get lucky... this one time... it might work.'

He gasps and swears loudly when I elbow him in the chest. I use the moment to scramble out of bed and pull my pants up.

'What on earth is your problem?' I shout.

A neighbour's dog barks somewhere in the distance – two dogs, I think. Maybe they can sense my distress.

The moonlight streaming in through the curtains casts a grey sheen over Edward's face, giving him a ghostly appearance.

He looks at me for a long time, then blinks and makes a sound in his throat.

'I'm so sorry, Sars,' he says, rolling onto his back, his eyes wide and staring up at the ceiling. 'I'm such a shit husband.' He groans and rubs his face. 'I thought everything might change... if, if we... my dad... he... oh God, I'm so sorry.'

'Hang on, did your dad say something to you about this on the weekend? When we first arrived?' I ask, folding my arms across my chest and taking a step away from the bed.

I've been meaning to find out what had gone on between Edward and Jeoffrey, but whenever I ask about it, Edward changes the subject.

Edward nods and wipes his wet face with the bedsheet. 'Yeah. He told me that if I... if we... don't give him a grandchild within the year, that he'll disinherit me.'

'Are you kidding me?' I say, trying my best to keep my voice calm. 'He really said that to you?' I lower myself on to the edge of the mattress.

'Yeah,' says Edward, his voice croaky.

'Doesn't he know how hellish this has been for us?' I shake my head. 'I mean, it's been so tough on us both.'

Edward shakes his head. 'You don't understand, Sars.

He said he has his reasons for wanting this. I think he might be sick. He's got heart problems. He wouldn't say exactly why he's so desperate. But he just wants a grandchild so badly.'

I stare out the bedroom window, at the long spindly branches of our tree in the front garden, stripped by the cool, harsh winds of autumn and winter. There'll be tiny buds of greenery popping up all over the branches soon. Though it's spring already, this tree has always been a late bloomer.

'He looked healthy though,' I say. 'He probably just wants his family name continued. And I understand how important that is to him, but…' I turn to face Edward. 'We just can't give him that. And we've tried so damn hard.' I shrug. 'Anyway, you and I have plenty of our own money. We don't need your parents' fortune.'

Edward says nothing and returns his gaze to the ceiling and smothers a sob with his hand.

'I don't deserve you,' he says. 'You deserve a better husband.'

'What are you talking about? We're going through a rough patch, that's all. What you did tonight is… well it wasn't nice, and I think you need to sleep off the booze in the spare room till morning. But I get why you tried, okay? I get it. Your dad is being a bully.'

'You don't understand though. He's got his reasons.'

'Screw his reasons,' I say. 'I'm calling him first thing in the morning and I'm going to tell him that we aren't having children anymore. That I don't want to risk dying just for a pile of old money and that we are perfectly fine without it.'

'What?' Edward practically leaps out of bed, instantly sobered. 'No. No you can't just call him and say that. Are you crazy? Promise me you won't.'

My husband's eyes are wild and bloodshot. He seems genuinely frightened.

'Okay. But let's talk about this in the morning,' I say,

feeling tired and blue all at once.

If only we could get past this. Move on and embrace life as a couple. Me and Edward against the world. Screw what his dad wants.

'I think we both need some sleep,' I say gently.

Edward nods. He takes a pillow under his arm, and, looking like a chastised child, disappears out of the room and down the hallway.

The sound of the spare bedroom door closing echoes into the quiet of the night, making me feel more alone than I've ever felt.

I reach for my phone and tap out a text to my mum.

But it doesn't deliver.

This doesn't bode well.

Either Bill has sold her phone to pay for his booze and cigarettes or Mum hasn't bothered to charge it. Which means she's not in a good state of mind.

I curl up into a ball on my side and cradle my phone to my chest, willing my mother to tap into her maternal instinct and somehow sense that I, her daughter, need help.

But I eventually fall asleep, clutching a silent phone.

16

Sara

When I wake early the next morning, before the sun is up, I slide my hand to my husband's side of the bed and feel around for him, surprised that he's not there.

But then I remember what happened and roll over onto my stomach and draw my pillow up around both sides of my head.

What has happened to us?

Why is my father-in-law, Jeoffrey, being such a jerk to Edward?

My bare skin prickles at the cool morning air so I throw on my soft white dressing gown and make my way into the kitchen for coffee.

It's a running joke between Edward and me, about my taste for instant coffee, and when I reach for the jar of granules, I'm surprised to find a yellow Post-it note stuck to the top.

> *I'm so sorry about last night. I'm going away for two nights to think, and to give you some space.*
> *Love you,*
> *Eddie*

I'm not sure how this note makes me feel. But after a few sips of coffee, I realise that time apart is probably a good thing and I'm grateful for the space to sort my head out.

After my second cup of coffee, my brain is sufficiently awake, and I decide it's time I did a little bit of investigating.

Edward has always prided himself on being the 'money man' as he calls himself and has used the excuse of 'it's too stressful' during my many short-lived pregnancies for not allowing me to take more of an active role in our personal bookkeeping.

But I'm not going to be getting pregnant anytime soon and it's about time I started to get involved in paying our bills and seeing where our money goes. There's no more sitting around being a kept woman for me.

The computer in our study doesn't have a password.

I don't personally use it much, as I generally do everything on my mobile phone or my laptop. But if I do use it, I usually read the news and search for random things, like recipes, while Edward uses it to look after our bills and manages our bank accounts, even mine.

I've always been okay with Edward having access to my finances because I've got nothing to hide. I'm a big believer in 'what's mine is yours'. But I've never thought to go on here and have a look at our money situation myself. I guess that's what happens when you finally have money in your life after years of living just below the poverty line. You give in to the comfort and don't even want to consider going back, or even think about it.

But perhaps checking in and getting to know my way around our financial situation, and where our money has been going, will at least set my mind at ease. I can make sure that Edward isn't doing anything in secret like having an affair and spending money on expensive hotel suites and designer lingerie for another woman to wear.

I turn on the computer, and while I wait for it to hum to life, what Stan told me last night plays on my mind. Does he actually believe that Neve and Edward would sleep with each other behind our backs? It's insane that he would even think it. Ludicrous.

Then I mull over what Neve told me last night, about her not wanting sex with Stan anymore. I mean, marital bedroom problems seem to be a common occurrence among couples with children – something I wouldn't know about, of course. But the more I think about it, the more I wonder if their marital issues run deeper.

Did Neve drink a bottle of prosecco before I arrived to give her the courage to tell me something else? Something she never got around to telling me because of Stan's interruption? If only Stan hadn't shown up and spoilt everything.

But no. I shake my head at my own stupidity. Neve said she can't even feel anything for the football player she has a crush on. She said that she feels 'blank' downstairs. The more I remember the conversation, and the look of sadness on Neve's face, the more I realise how ridiculous Stan's cheating accusations sound.

And I've stupidly let him get inside my head.

Neve is my best friend and Edward my husband.

They would never betray me.

The computer makes a bleeping sound, as a blank screen with a small window asks for a password.

This can't be right. This computer has never been password-protected.

I googled a recipe for dinner only a couple of weeks ago and it didn't ask for a password back then.

I try every birthdate and name combination I can think of, but no such luck.

Eventually, after several more tries, I give up and decide to clean the house. Hopefully the chores will distract me from my increasingly paranoid thoughts about my husband and whether he's hiding something from me.

An hour later, I'm sitting in the living room, waiting for the floors to dry, the house smelling as fresh as a pine forest, when there's a knock at my front door.

I kick off my slippers and make my way to the door, leaping across the damp tiles in my socks.

'Mum,' I say, completely taken by surprise, when I see her standing on my front doorstep through the screen door. 'What... um... why are you here?'

'Hello to you too, Sara,' says Mum, a twinkle in her eye.

She has an overnight bag hanging from one arm, and a bag of groceries dangling from the other.

'I've come to stay for a couple of days. Or for as long as you need me,' she says, her face crinkling into a smile.

'Oh, wow, um, that's so great.' I open the door and take the groceries and the overnight bag from her arms and step back to allow her through. 'Sorry, I'm just in shock. Come in.'

Mum steps inside, her eyes wide as she admires the high ceilings and ornate cornices as though for the first time.

She doesn't come over much. Usually just for Christmas and Easter. I'm always inviting her over to stay for longer spans of time, but she always declines because she likes her own space and loves her little apartment.

The only exception was when I became very weak after my last pregnancy loss. She did stay for a week back then, which I appreciated. But even then, I could sense her need to retreat to her own space by the end of the week.

'What about Bill?' I ask, heaving the groceries onto the kitchen counter and setting the overnight bag on the floor.

Mum snorts and waves a hand in the air at the mention of the man.

'I've given him two nights to sort himself out. I told him he needs to be gone by the time I'm back or I'm calling the police.'

'Wow. Go you,' I say and give Mum a spontaneous hug, breathing in her familiar scent of Tabu perfume and the same rose-scented shampoo she's been using since forever. 'I'm so proud of you, Mum.'

She hugs me back and when we part to unpack the groceries, she grins.

'You should have seen his face. He looked like he wanted to slap me but luckily Beryl from next door was over at the time, dropping off her Tupperware catalogue. I think he likes her.'

'Oh God, well let's hope she doesn't like him back. The last thing you need is for Bill to be living next door to you.'

Mum laughs.

'Beryl? No chance of that. She's got a girlfriend who lives with her. Annette. She sells Avon. They do their parties together and are a very successful couple. They're buying a house in the country one day.' Mum laughs again. 'Beryl detests Bill. I think the Tupperware catalogue was a ruse to check if I was okay.'

'Gosh, well I'm glad for the Beryls of the world,' I say, my heart bursting with gratitude to have my mother here with me in my kitchen, an overnight bag filled for a couple nights' stay.

'Maybe we can catch a movie tomorrow,' Mum says. 'And go out for a nice lunch at that Beach Bar Café.'

At the mention of the café my face falls and Mum notices.

'But first things first,' says Mum, her face growing serious. 'How about I make us some tea and we sit outside in the back garden to catch up on what's been happening with you?'

Everything that has been bothering me rises and lodges in my throat, and for a moment I'm unable to speak. To finally have an opportunity to get it all off my chest, seems too good to be true.

Mum frowns.

'I know it's a shock to see me here, love, because I haven't always been there for you. And while I can't undo what I've done in the past, I'm going to give it my best shot to support you right now.' She slides her hand across the counter and lightly brushes the tips of my fingers with her own. 'So you're stuck with me.'

My throat tightens with emotion. But I'm not going to waste a single, precious moment with Mum by crying. The good times with my mother have been so few and far between.

From experience, I've learned that my relationship with her can be snatched away at any given moment by a human parasite. Because for some reason, Mum is a magnet for cruel men who treat her horribly and drain her of not only her spirit but her time and money.

'How did you know I needed you? I messaged you but it wouldn't deliver.'

Mum sighs and a dark look crosses her face.

'That bastard Bill sold my phone for a pizza and a packet of cigarettes. But anyway, the landlord dropped in early this morning. Brian. He lives on site. He's a good man.' Mum's expression softens.

'That's good to hear. But I don't understand what your landlord has got to do with you knowing that I needed you.'

'Well, how about you let me finish,' she says, her voice taking on a mock-stern tone.

I put my palms up and laugh. 'Okay, okay.'

'Edward contacted the landlord's office and left an urgent message for me to drop everything and come to see you.' Mum shrugs and raises her brows. 'So I packed my bag, gave Bill the ultimatum, and here I am.'

'You chose me over Bill,' I say, unsure I can believe it. 'And Edward arranged all of it?'

'Of course I did. And I always will.' She makes a face. 'Sure, I let him into my home in a moment of weakness, but I'm going to do my best to never let that happen again.' Mum beams a smile my way. 'And as for your darling husband, yes, he's the one who asked me to come.'

'Wow,' I say, and sit down on the stool by the bench, watching while Mum busies herself in the kitchen boiling the kettle and dropping teabags into my favourite forest-green handmade mugs.

Once we're outside, sitting beneath the huge old almond tree that grows in the yard, while pretty, pink and white blossoms flutter to the ground and onto our laps, I tell my mother everything about Edward and his parents.

'Why on earth is Jeoffrey being so petty?' she asks, sipping the last of her tea, before cradling the empty mug in her wrinkled hands. 'I can't believe he tried to blackmail Edward with money. Rich old bastard.'

'Mum,' I say, unable to hide my grin. 'He's not that bad. Apparently, he has "his reasons" according to Edward.'

Mum sighs and raises her brows.

'I guess it explains why Edward is so determined to give it another go, but it still doesn't excuse him for going too far last night.'

'No. Of course not,' I say. 'But I've forgiven him. And as long as we can move forward from this... this horrible phase, I'm happy to put it in the past where it belongs.'

'That's kind of you,' Mum says, looking pensive and studying a snowy blossom that's landed on her arm. 'I know I've forgiven my fair share of men in my time. Although some of them shouldn't have been forgiven.'

'All of them, you mean.'

'True,' Mum agrees with a wry smile. 'But Edward isn't like any of those men. He's different. He has a kind heart. And it's obvious that his father has been manipulating him with money this whole time and... he must have gotten desperate last night.' Mum gives me a knowing look. 'As long as he doesn't do it again.'

I recall the way he sobbed after I yelled at him to stop.

'Yeah, well, I'd say he won't be doing that again.' I shrug. 'But as for the money, we have heaps of our own. So I don't know why Edward is letting his dad get to him.'

'There must be more to the story,' Mum says, rubbing her chin.

'Maybe. I wanted to call Jeoffrey and find out why he's being this way, but Edward begged me not to. I promised him I wouldn't.'

Mum's eyes twinkle with mischief.

‘Well I haven’t made any promises, have I? How about I call Edith and find out what’s going on with Jeoffrey and Eddie for you? She’ll know for sure. And she likes me. Last Christmas we got on like a house on fire, remember?’

‘I think that was the champagne, Mum,’ I say, raising a single brow.

Mum waves a dismissive hand at me and gets up, disappearing inside the house.

I follow her in and find her on my home phone in the kitchen, my no-longer-used address book open in front of her.

‘Hello, Jeoffrey, this is Carmella here ... Yes, I’m good thank you. May I please speak with Edith? ... Oh, not until tonight? ... Oh. Okay. Perhaps I can speak with you then, if you have a minute ... Yes. It’s about Edward and Sara ... No. Nobody asked me to call ... I wanted to know for myself why you’re bullying my daughter about something she has no control over ... Yes. I see ... What possible reason could you have? ... Well, I understand your need for privacy, but it does affect my daughter and ... Okay. Okay I’ll let it go for now ... Yes ... Yes, I’m worried too. But if you could tell me what’s behind it all then I can help ... Just try me, I might know how to help ... Well, okay then ... Goodbye.’

My mother ends the call and hangs the phone back on the kitchen wall.

‘He said he can’t divulge why he’s being so hard on Edward, on you both. But there’s a reason behind it all, apparently. Two reasons. But he said he needs his privacy respected on the matter.’ Mum gives me a knowing look and softens her voice. ‘Jeoffrey said he’s worried about Edward, love. He said that there are things that you, Sara, are unaware of. But he also said that he’s not in position to tell you what exactly. He said that Edward needs to be the one to tell you.’

At my mother’s words, my paranoia kicks up a notch.

Could Jeoffrey know what's behind Edward's recent change of behaviour?

A few minutes later, while I'm handwashing the cups in the sink, and still thinking about what Jeoffrey said on the phone, Mum enters the kitchen.

'There's a kid at the door for you,' she says, frowning. 'He looks about fifteen or sixteen.'

'Oh really?' I ask.

'He said his name is Harley.'

17

@MrSugarDaddy111

I'm at a hotel right now. You should come see me.

What's in it for me?

A good time and maybe a few treats.

What kind of treats? You better mean money or I'm blocking you.

Hmmm, depends how good you are for Daddy.

Cringe.

You really are a baby, you know that?

Well, I am only seventeen, so...

You said you were eighteen last night.

Oops. My bad. Do you still want me to come?

Sure.

You are so baaaad. What's the hotel and room number? And you need to send me money for an Uber.

Send me a photo of your breasts first. So that I know you're serious.

No way. And who the hell says breasts?

Fine. Goodbye.

An hour later...

Good girl. I like the pic you sent. The room is 106 at the Hotel Stanton. I'll give you cash for your Uber when you arrive.

What should I wear?

Anything. It doesn't matter. I have a dress for you to put on for me.

Do you buy all your sugar babies

dresses? Or am I your first baby?

What do you think?

I don't know. I guess you've probably had heaps of girls.

You're right. But my old baby, well, she broke... so I need a new one.

Haha, that sounds so wrong. I hope you don't break me ;)

We'll see. If you're a good baby, you'll be just fine.

What do you mean by 'just fine'? Are you going to hurt me?

I guess you'll find out when you meet me.

18

Sara

'Harley. How do you know where I live?'

The boy on my doorstep backs away, his mouth a tight line.

'Sorry. I wanted a drink of water, but I'll just go.'

I take a step out, my fingers resting on the doorknob. The sun is out now, piercing through the clouds and near-blinding me. I raise a hand to shield my eyes.

'No, wait. I'm sorry,' I say, when he turns to face me. 'I'm just... surprised to see you here, that's all.'

Harley nods and I notice that his eyes are red and puffy, as though he's been crying.

'Are you okay, Harley?'

He rubs his face and turns away from me so that he's facing the street.

'No, I'm not.' There's a tremor to his voice that breaks my heart. 'Everything's bad... it's...'

'It's what?' I ask gently.

He shakes his head. The poor kid. His pain is so great he can't even speak.

I'm not even sure what to do right now. The only experience with teens I have is with Liv, and she's not talking to me right now. So maybe I'm not cut out for this. Maybe helping kids isn't for me.

But I need to try something. Harley obviously needs my help.

'Whatever it is that is bothering you, I'm sure it'll pass. And in the meantime, I'm happy to help you in any way. Even if it's just to listen.'

He half turns and looks at me from the corner of his eye.

'You're nice,' he says. 'There's a lot of shitty people around. People who don't give a crap.'

'Has something happened, Harley?'

His eyes well with tears and he turns away again and watches a shiny red car disappear down the street.

'Yeah, something bad. Something very bad.'

'Where are your parents?' I ask, my stomach churning with foreboding. 'Are you still living at home?'

'Yeah. But they're not the same. Just in their room most of the time.'

'What do you mean by *not the same*?' I ask.

Harley shrugs.

'I'm going now,' he says, his throat croaky. 'I just wanted to…' He shakes his head and backs away. 'This is a mistake. I should never have come.'

'Wait. Please. I want to help you, Harley, but I'm not sure how. Please let me know what you need.'

'It's okay. Don't worry,' he says, before he turns and starts walking away.

'Wait. You said you wanted a drink of water. Can I at least get you that before you go?'

He pauses, his back to me for a long time, before he turns back around.

'Okay. Yeah. Thanks. And can I use your bathroom?'

I let him in and show him to the guest bathroom. My mother is nowhere to be seen.

'Take as long as you like,' I say. 'I'll pour you a drink. Just water or would you like some lemonade or orange juice?'

'Water is fine,' he says and closes the door to the bathroom.

The poor kid. He is going through something tough.

I head into the kitchen and from the window I can see that my mother has returned to sit beneath the almond tree. She looks so old, but so at peace sitting there with her eyes closed as the blossoms flutter around her. She makes such a pretty picture I wish I had my phone with me to take a pic. But instead I savour the moment.

Standing up to Bill and coming here has changed something in her. It's likely the first time she's stood up to a man and had her say, laid out her terms.

'Hey.'

I turn around and smile at Harley.

'I'm sorry, I was deep in thought,' I say.

He shrugs and half-smiles. 'It's okay. My mum does that all the time.'

'What's your mum like?' I ask as I pour him a glass of

water from the filtered tap.

Harley takes the water and gulps half of it down in one go.

'She's nice,' he says, taking a breath. 'You'd like her.'

'And what about your dad?'

Harley shrugs. 'He's okay. I think he's got depression. He hasn't worked since I was born. Work accident, I think. But the company's got some expensive lawyers and said it was his fault.'

'That's awful,' I say, wondering if Edward has some contacts in law that I could pass on to Harley's family. 'Things must be tough at home, then,' I probe.

Harley blinks and his fingers twitch. For a second, I think he's going to drop the glass of water to the floor, but he exhales and then sets it down on the counter.

'Thanks for the water,' he says and turns to leave.

But as he walks down the hallway to the front door, he glances to his left, where wedding photos of Edward and me decorate the wall, then stops and does a double take.

'Oh, our wedding photos,' I say, even though it's obvious from the big white dress and tuxedo.

'So that *is* your husband,' Harley says quietly, a deep frown creasing his brow.

'Yes. His name is Edward.'

Harley's dark eyes study my husband's face intensely. His jaw stiffens.

'What's the matter?' I ask, the pulse in my ears growing louder. Harley's interest in my husband is downright strange. 'Do you know my husband?'

Harley blinks rapidly at the photo and then takes a backwards step and trips on my foot.

I reach out to steady him, but he leaps back as though my touch has burned his skin.

'Get away from me,' he shouts, pressing himself up against the wall so that he can be as far away from me as possible.

'Hey, what's wrong?'

Harley bolts towards the screen door, crashing into it. He fiddles with the latch, but in his haste, locks it instead of unlocking it.

'Let me get it for you,' I say, keeping my voice as soft and as calm as possible. I approach Harley and the door with caution. 'Just please stay calm. I'm letting you out right now.'

As I near him, he flinches, as though I'm going to hurt him. It's so confusing, but right now what matters is that Harley feels safe.

I unlock the door and fling it open for him, then stand back.

As soon as I do, Harley bolts out the door and onto the street, without a backward glance.

'What did that boy want?' my mum asks when I join her in the yard a few minutes later.

'I'm not sure,' I say, my heart still racing from what just happened. 'I think he wanted help.'

'What was all that shouting about?' she asks.

'Oh, nothing really.' I shrug. 'You know teenage boys, they get pretty rowdy,' I say and force a smile.

But it wasn't nothing.

Harley was scared.

And he recognised my husband.

The question is, from where?

19

Sara

I decide not to tell Edward about Harley's visit while he is away. Because I need a bit of time to digest what happened myself first, and there is only so much you can convey over text anyway. Also a phone call would defeat the purpose of our time apart. We need this space. This distance. So that we can better appreciate each other, or perhaps better appreciate ourselves.

Another thing, this is something I need to tell him when he gets home, face to face, so that I can watch him closely and gauge his reaction at the mention of Harley.

Plus, for selfish reasons, I want to forget all about my husband, and Harley's weird and unsettling visit, and just enjoy my last day with Mum before she heads back to her apartment. There will be plenty of time to have a serious chat with Edward about everything once he comes home and Mum returns to her flat.

So for the next twenty-four hours, Mum and I make the most of our time together.

We go to the movies and watch a sappy film that has us emerge from the darkened cinema and onto the sunny streets with red eyes and blotchy faces from crying.

But we are soon laughing when we spy our tragic reflections in a shop window. I haven't laughed like that in ages.

On the walk back to the car, Mum insists that we stop and enter Funzone, where she wins me a soft toy on a claw machine. It's as though she's trying to make up for all the missed time we should have had together when I was younger.

But I'm not complaining. It is nice to have Mum fuss over me.

After a late dinner at the Beach Bar Café – which my mother insists she pay for with her pension, despite me begging her to let me cover it – we arrive home yawning in unison.

'I'm exhausted,' Mum says, yawning. 'Do you mind if I get an early night? I've got to get the early bus tomorrow morning.'

'Not at all. I'm tired, too. It's gone by so quickly,' I say, hanging my keys on the hook and setting my handbag on the kitchen counter. 'And forget the bus, I'll take you. Have a sleep in and then when you're ready I'll drive you home.'

Mum's eyes crinkle up at the corners. 'Thanks, love.' She covers her mouth as she yawns again. 'Okay. Well, I'm off to bed. Thank you for the most magical two days,' she says, her voice breaking a little as she opens her arms and sweeps me in for a hug.

'It's been so great having you here,' I say, wishing that she could stay longer. Now that I have Mum in my life it seems I can't get enough of her company. And maybe that's because I need her right now more than ever.

* * *

The next morning, I drive Mum home, and when we arrive at her apartment block, I follow her upstairs, bracing myself for an altercation with Bill.

Thankfully though, Beryl from next door informs Mum that Bill has done a runner.

'The police came asking for him after a tip-off about

his sticky fingers,' says Beryl, winking at us both. 'He's been helping himself to other people's belongings, not just yours, Carmella. So I don't think he'll be back anytime soon. Everyone wants a piece of him.'

'Good riddance to that man,' says Mum, before turning to me and hugging me tightly. 'Thank you, Sara. You take care of yourself and call me tonight. Let me know how things are after Edward gets home.'

'Will do. You take care too.'

'Annette and I will look after your mum, so don't you worry,' says Beryl, her cherry red hair glinting in the morning sun.

I nod my thanks and leave.

While driving home, I get a call from Neve.

My stomach swirls with dread as my index finger hovers over the answer button on my handsfree.

The past twenty-four hours with Mum felt like a holiday in a sense, a getaway from my life. It was easy to forget all my worries while seated in the plush red velvet chairs of the movie theatre, shovelling popcorn into my mouth.

Now I'm not so sure I'm ready to go back to spending every minute consumed with suspicion and worries.

I stare at the phone and finally accept the call.

Time to face the real world, Sara.

'Sara?' Neve's voice sounds so small and faraway.

'Hey, Neve, you're on speakerphone. I'm driving back from Mum's. Can you hear me?'

'Sara,' she says, ignoring my question and sounding panicked, 'I need to tell you everything. I can't do this anymore. I need to tell you about Liv...' Her voice trails off and she begins to sob.

'What's happened?' I ask, my heart racing. 'You're scaring me.'

'She hates me... and it's all because of him. It's all because of him. I should never... I should never have said yes... I should never have agreed...' She starts to cry again.

'Neve,' I say, trying to keep my voice calm while I steer my car off the road and into a resting bay on the side of the highway. Once I'm parked, I turn off the engine and lock my doors. 'Start from the beginning. Tell me about Liv. I'm listening.'

There's a long pause on the other end.

'Oh... oh gosh, I'm so stupid. My meds... they've got me feeling weird.'

'Wait, what meds? And they shouldn't make you feel weird. They should make you feel good. What were you going to say? About Liv.'

'Stan... he's coming now. Should be home any minute. He was on... a business trip. But he said he'd... take me to the doctors, I think. You know... to change my medication. I don't feel right, Sara... not the same.'

'Then you should get that checked out right now. But what about Liv? What do you mean by "him"? Whose fault is it? Do you mean Stan?'

'Stan?' Neve says, her voice sounding strange, as though she's already forgotten what she'd said.

A road train pulls off the highway and slowly chugs past me, its engine hissing loudly when it comes to a stop, blocking out some of what Neve is saying.

'No... home. He's... now... he has been really...'

'Do you want me to come over? I'm about half an hour away,' I say, my heart racing in alarm.

'No,' she says quickly. 'I won't be here.'

Then the call disconnects.

20

Sara

By the time I pull up at home after dropping Mum off, I'm still rattled by Neve's call. It doesn't help that she didn't answer the phone when I called her back and hasn't responded to any of my text messages asking if she needs to speak to me privately.

Edward pulls into the driveway just as I'm getting out of my car.

'Hey,' he says, whipping off his sunglasses and beaming a huge smile as he gets out of the vehicle. He unsuccessfully hides a bunch of colourful flowers behind his back. 'Did you miss me?'

Though I'd planned on staying a little cool towards my husband for the next few days, the sight of him, after him being gone for two nights, immediately uplifts me, and reminds me of how much I need and love Edward.

'Of course I did,' I say, shoving my keys in my pockets and running to him. Everything right now is so uncertain, and seeing Edward is like being anchored back into the familiar.

He opens his arms wide, flowers in one hand, and when I fall into his embrace, tears prickle my eyes. Things have been so strange lately. And a deep feeling at the base of my gut tells me that the worst is yet to come.

'God, I missed you,' he says, hugging me so tightly to him that I can feel his thudding heart against my own.

'There's so much I want to tell you.'

'Me too,' I say, glancing over at our next-door neighbour, Ron, who is hand-watering his front garden with a hose and pretending not to notice us. 'Actually, let's get inside first. I have heaps to tell you.'

As soon as we're inside and Edward has placed the flowers in the sink, he turns to me and takes my hand, tugging me toward the living room where we sit on the couch.

'I've had a lot of time to think,' says Edward, after clearing his throat. 'And I'm going to go visit my parents. I'm going to tell my father that I don't care about the inheritance. That you and I have decided not to have children, and that we don't need their money. We have plenty of our own.'

He shakes his head and his gaze drifts to the carpeted floor for a few seconds, before he finally looks up. 'And I promise you, that what I did to you the other night, will never ever happen again. I am so, so sorry for how I behaved. It was... it's unforgivable.'

I stare into my husband's dark green eyes. The two nights away have done him good. His skin is no longer flushed and the deep crease in his forehead has softened.

'Thank you,' I say, taking his hand in mine. 'I forgive you and I believe you. I know you won't ever do that again.'

He presses my hand to his lips and sighs, his breath warm against my skin.

'Thank you, thank you, thank you, Sara. Things are going to be different from now on. I promise.'

I notice that Edward's phone hasn't beeped once since he's arrived home.

'Your phone,' I say, deciding now's as good as any time to bring it up. 'It's always beeping. And you're always hiding away in the garage or the bathroom with it.'

Edward rubs the back of his neck and licks his lips.

'All things of the past. You don't have to worry about that anymore. I've... I'm... we're okay now. My phone won't be beeping anymore. I promise you.'

I stare at him for a long time and decide that in order to have a fresh start, we need as much honesty as possible between us.

'Was it another woman?' I ask, Stan's words echoing in the back of my mind.

Edward widens his eyes, as though he's completely surprised by my question, then he laughs.

'No. Oh God, Sara, no. There's no way I would ever, *ever* cheat on you. Trust me on this.' He shakes his head and presses his lips to my hand several times. 'There will never be another woman in my life. There's only you. It's only ever been you.'

Edward holds my gaze. He doesn't even blink. My gut instinct tells me he's being truthful.

Now what Stan told me about his suspicions of Neve and Edward having an affair seems genuinely absurd.

'Okay,' I say. 'I believe you. But it still doesn't explain you and your phone.'

He lets go of my hand and takes his phone out of the inside pocket of his jacket.

'Here. Take it for as long as you like. You won't find any sign of an affair. Those pings were... they were work-related, and I've put a stop to them. From now on, you are my priority. You're my family, Sara, my best friend, my wife. You're my number one. From now on, let's be totally honest with each other. Everything else is in the past, where it belongs.'

I can't help but notice that Edward hardly took a breath while he made all those promises. It feels a little rushed and impulsive, and... not right.

'Stan came to see me,' I blurt out, because if we're coming clean then I'd rather Edward knows about his best friend's visit now and not later.

Edward's body turns rigid, but he catches me noticing and exhales, relaxing his body. It's a strange reaction. I wonder what that's all about?

'What did he want?' he asks, forcing himself to sound as light and as casual as possible. But I can tell that he's apprehensive.

I watch my husband's face extra closely.

'He said that he's worried about you. That you have secrets. He thought you might be having an affair with Neve.'

My husband draws his head back and blinks rapidly. He appears genuinely shocked at the suggestion. He's either a wonderful actor or is being completely transparent.

'Why on earth would he say something like that? It's totally ridiculous. Me and Neve?' Edward screws his face up at the idea. 'When did you see him?'

'The night before you left. He came to see me after I'd met with Neve at the café. I texted you, but didn't get a chance to tell you about it properly because you came home late and then...'

Edward grimaces. 'I came home drunk and behaved like an absolute arsehole and a monster. I'm sorry.'

'Look, I actually don't believe what Stan said. But I am worried about Neve.'

I tell him about the phone call from Neve, how she cried and said things about Liv and then did a complete about-face and blamed her meds for what she was saying.

'That's odd.' He shakes his head. 'But I'm guessing she's probably having a tough time with Liv being gone. Stan too. Maybe that's why he's saying all this weird stuff.' Edward shrugs. 'I guess all couples go through tough times,' he says, giving me a knowing look, which then turns into a half-smile. 'Even us.'

His smile melts me, a tiny bit, and I offer a flicker of a smile in return.

'True.' But still, I can't get the haunting sound of Neve crying out of my head. 'Can you at least call Stan and ask how Neve is? I've texted and called her, but I get no response. I'm worried. Especially now that Lawrence is staying with them. She told me he watches her and gives her the creeps.'

Edward frowns. He seems as concerned as I am. Good.

'As soon as I get my bag out of the car and unpack, I'll give Stan a call. I'm sure everything is fine. You know Neve, she can get a bit dramatic sometimes.'

'You didn't hear her,' I say. 'She sounded distraught.'

Edward gets up and bends to peck my forehead.

'That must have been awful for you. I'll call Stan soon. And if I can't get through to him, then we'll drive over to their house together, okay? But I'm sure everything is fine and it's all a misunderstanding.'

'Maybe,' I say, but I find that hard to believe.

21

Sara

Twenty minutes later, Edward gives me a thumbs up while he holds the phone to his ear. The frown lines have disappeared from his forehead, and when he smiles at me reassuringly, it gives me hope.

'They're at the doctor's getting her meds checked out as we speak,' Edward says, to me, before getting back to Stan. 'Oh, okay. Well that sounds positive,' he says, tilting the phone away from his mouth. 'Stan says that the doctor is going to switch her meds. Neve will call you back tonight and explain everything. And she's feeling better by the way and hopes she didn't scare you before. She's very sorry, Stan says.'

'Please tell Neve that she never has to apologise. Tell her I can't wait to hear from her tonight.'

Edward nods and passes on my message to Stan. I'm hoping it gets to Neve. But regardless of what Stan tells her, I aim to speak to her tonight. If she doesn't call me, then I'll call her and keep trying until I reach her.

I mouth a 'thank you' and take my car keys off the hook and grab my handbag. I've decided to celebrate Edward's return home, and the fact that he's promised positive changes in our relationship, by making a lasagne.

Edward waves me off from the kitchen as I leave to shop for groceries.

But when I step out the front door, I freeze on the spot.

I have a visitor.

'Harley, what are you doing here again?' I ask, a wave of panic washing over me. With Edward's return and the whole Neve situation, I'd almost forgotten about Harley.

Harley tucks a lock of hair behind his ear with trembling nail-bitten fingers, and sucks in a deep breath.

'I need to talk to you about your husband.'

Harley's words turn my blood cold, chasing away all the warmth my husband's promises and flowers had given me.

I glance over my shoulder. Edward's voice drifts out through the open window. He's still on the phone with Stan in the kitchen.

'You need to make it quick,' I say, a feeling of dread already building in my stomach. 'He's inside.'

We walk towards my car.

'I've got sisters,' he says. 'One of them, Dani. She's always... she *was* always wanting me to study at school so I can get a good job and to not make the same mistakes she did when she flunked all her classes.'

I nod, wondering where this is going and how his sister is connected to my husband.

'She even dobbed me into my parents two weeks ago, when she caught me wagging school and washing windows instead. But it was because she...' Harley's chin begins to wobble and he looks away, staring at our next-door neighbour's garden. 'She cared.'

My heart softens and I forget Edward for a moment.

'She sounds like such a great sister,' I say, but my skin prickles with goosebumps and I shiver, despite the warm sun shining its brightest today. Why is he using the past tense? Did she run away? Like Liv?

'But when she dobbed me into my parents, I got so mad, I snuck into her room while she was in the shower. Anyway, I knew the passcode to her phone.'

Harley meets my gaze and shrugs, his cheeks tinting pink.

'It's a little trick I learnt just by watching people's fingers moving over the keys. I'm good at it. I know lots of strangers' passcodes too,' he says knowingly, 'just from watching them at the lights while I wash their windows.'

He had better not be implying that he knows mine. I want to admonish him for invading people's privacy like that, but I say nothing because I sense what he's about to tell me is important.

'I got into her phone and found out that her boyfriend was cheating on her. This guy she works with at Val's Burgers. His name is Flynn and I hate him.'

'That's awful,' I say. 'And Flynn is an idiot. Your sister sounds like a great person.'

'Yeah. But then I saw that she was talking to

someone new, on Instagram. His username is @MrSugarDaddy111. I think she was just talking to him to try and make Flynn jealous… to get him back.'

'Sounds like a creep,' I say, rubbing at the goosebumps that continue to prickle my arms. This is getting a little strange. Why is Harley telling me all of this?

Harley looks at me sharply then, intently, as if reading my mind, and I feel exposed, as though his gaze has opened me up and he's had a bit of rummage inside my soul.

'I took a photo of their conversation using my phone, because I wanted something over her, so she wouldn't dob on me to my parents again for wagging school.'

I nod. 'I can understand that. But you shouldn't have invaded her privacy. I bet she's not happy about it.'

Harley blinks rapidly.

'It doesn't matter now.'

'Why doesn't it matter, Harley?'

He swallows thickly.

'Because she's dead.'

It takes me a few seconds to process what I just heard.

'Oh, no. Oh… Harley… I'm so sorry to hear that,' I say. After a few seconds of intense silence, I can't help but ask. 'How did it happen?'

Harley stares at me in disbelief.

'Haven't you seen the news?'

My head feels light. The news? And then it dawns on me. Oh. My. God.

'Your sister is *Danielle Stokes*?'

He nods and looks at the ground, kicking at the gap between the brick pavers where green moss has started to grow.

'Oh, Harley. That's… oh God, I'm so sorry.'

He puts a hand up, to silence my condolences. He's probably sick of people telling him how sorry they are.

Sorry isn't going to bring back his big sister.

'In the beginning, when she first went missing, we thought she'd gone back to Flynn. She used to do that. Take a bag of clothes and go sleep at his place for a few weeks. I mean, she is twenty. Was. But now... now that I know she's been murdered... well, I think this guy she was talking to online probably has something to do with it.'

'Have you told your parents? The police?'

He shakes his head.

'I wanted to come to you first. Before I tell them.'

'Why me?' I ask, completely perplexed, and maybe a little bit touched that he chose me to help him, out of all the people that he knows.

Harley looks me in the eye and then takes his phone out of his back pocket and swipes it open.

'Because the man my sister was talking to is your husband. Your husband is @MrSugarDaddy111.'

'What?' Blood drains from my face and I instantly feel faint.

Harley holds the phone out, and when I see the familiar face on the screen I inhale sharply, my breath trapped in my throat.

Edward's face stares back at me.

It's a photo from a trip to Melbourne we'd taken a couple of years ago with Neve and Stan. My husband looks so happy and carefree, so alive.

I take the phone out of Harley's hand and zoom in.

'Where did you get this photo?'

Harley sighs with frustration. 'I told you. I took a screenshot of my sister's phone. This is who she was talking to. Your husband. The same man in your wedding photo.'

'But why would someone use my husband's photo?' I say, my heart beating like a drum against my chest. 'Neither of us has ever posted this... my husband doesn't even have social media... so I don't know how they would have…'

Harley takes his phone back and shoves it in his back pocket.

'Ask him. Ask him if he knows anything about my sister. They were arranging to meet. He might know something.'

He might have killed her, is what Harley is really saying.

The oats I've eaten for breakfast swirl in my stomach, threatening to come back up the way they went in.

'Is this why you followed me home that first time? Did you know all along?'

Harley nods. 'I saw him once, in your car. I expected you when I approached his window, but it was him.'

My throat tightens and my mouth fills with saliva.

I'm going to be sick.

'Sit down. You look pale,' says Harley, grabbing a hold of my arm. 'I'm sorry.'

'Don't be,' I say, feeling slightly better sitting on the concrete beside my car.

Harley takes a step back.

'You need to talk to your husband. Please. I need answers.'

I glance up at him and shield my eyes from the sun. 'I'll try my best. I… this is all just a… complete shock. I'm sure there's an explanation,' I say, but my mouth fills with saliva and I force my breakfast back down.

Ron from next door watches us for a bit, and looks me in the eye, hesitating, his mouth half open. I think he wants to ask if I'm okay, so I wave at him and paste a fake smile on my face. He seems satisfied with that, nods, then disappears inside his home.

'I'll give you a bit of time… I don't know, to get over the shock of it.' Harley tugs his backpack over his shoulder. 'I'm going to my usual spot to wash windows. Meet me there in an hour. If you don't show…' – he pauses and narrows his gaze – 'I'm going straight to the police.'

22

Neve

'Doctor's orders,' says Stan, blocking out the warm sunlight streaking in through the bedroom window and casting a dark shadow over me.

I open my mouth to protest, but Stan raises a palm in the air to shush me.

'And you don't have to worry about Jake because I've taken the rest of the day off, and the rest of the week for that matter. So you can relax and take it easy.'

I take the two slim white pills that I've never seen before from his open palm and toss them into my mouth before taking a sip from the glass of water he's left for me on the bedside table.

'Good. I'll go get your lunch,' he says, before he turns and leaves.

While he's gone, I spit out the pills and hide them in my pillowcase. I'll have to remember to get rid of them, flush them down the toilet. I wouldn't put it past Stan to check. He's been acting so odd lately. Controlling. As though he wants to lock me away.

It makes me think he has something to hide. Something he doesn't want me to find out about. My normally good-natured, calm husband has transformed over the past few weeks. And it's ever since that night, when I stupidly made that suggestion to Stan.

Honestly, I feel like everything went wrong after that night.

Stan became a different person – a stressed out, emotional and clingy husband.

And Liv left home.

I groan out loud and clutch at the bedcovers.

My heart aches at the thought of my daughter.

Oh Liv, where are you?

Stan returns with my lunch and as I move my fork around the lumpy mashed potato, I wonder if he'd go so far as to drug my food.

At the doctor's he seemed a bit pushy, suggesting various medications that I haven't even heard of. I'm glad the doctor politely asked Stan to leave so that she could speak to me in private.

I'm not sure what those pills are that Stan tried to give me, because the doctor didn't write me a script. And there were no 'doctor's orders' other than to go easy on myself. She was a very understanding woman.

In private, I told her about Liv, and the doctor had empathised, being a mother herself. She gave me hope after telling me that she once had a wayward teenage daughter who is now a successful and happy young woman in her twenties.

So I guess I should be thanking Stan for taking me there today, because I do feel a little more hopeful about Liv.

But as for Stan…

I'm getting more concerned as time goes by.

'Thanks for this,' I say, smiling up at him.

My words seem to relax him, and he sinks onto the edge of the bed and rubs his face.

'Sorry I haven't been myself, Neve.' He shakes his head. 'I've been worried about Eddie and Sara, and Liv of course, and… I guess I haven't been looking after you enough. But that's going to change. You're my wife,' he says, his voice cracking as his hand blindly reaches for mine.

When he finds my fingers, he gives them a squeeze.

'We're soulmates,' he says. 'I don't ever want to lose you.'

I'm surprised at the depth of my husband's feelings, at his sudden neediness. It both scares me and touches me. I've never seen such vulnerability in my husband before.

'You'll never lose me, Stan. I took those vows seriously,' I say, giving his hand a squeeze back.

Stan's phone beeps, with not one, but two messages.

'Is that Liv?' I ask, feeling jealous that he is the one privy to her messages.

My husband glances at his phone and his cheeks turn pink.

'No... it's... a work issue,' he says, before getting up and leaving without a backward glance.

23

Sara

After Harley is gone, I take a few minutes to compose myself and to calm my racing heart.

Birds flit across the sky and the sun continues to shine. Neighbour Ron's colourful petunias sway prettily in the gentle breeze. But here I am, finding it difficult to breathe, let alone think.

No amount of thinking or problem-solving is going to

get me out of what I need to do right now, which is confront my husband. So I force myself to my feet, and drag myself into my house, even though I'd much rather turn around and walk away, from this house, from Edward, from everything.

Because I don't want to know. I don't want to accept the possibility that my husband has been writing to the young woman who was murdered and given a watery grave.

'Edward?' I call out, because I can no longer hear him talking on the phone. 'Where are you?'

My voice sounds strange, strangled and high-pitched over my pulse, which sounds like a rushing river. And every time I blink, I see spots in front of my eyes. I must have been staring at the sun for too long.

'Here,' he says.

I jump at the sound of his voice and turn to find my husband standing behind me in the hallway.

He looks normal. An average looking thirty-something husband. Calmer and less frazzled today than he's been the past few months.

I can't help but stare at him, searching for the other side of him. The dark side.

Could this man be @MrSugarDaddy111?

And could he be responsible for killing Harley's sister?

'Why are you looking at me like that?' he says, taking a step towards me and lightly brushing his fingers along my forearm.

My skin prickles with goosebumps and I pull my arm away from his touch. It's involuntary. I can't help it after what Harley showed me.

'Have you... had you been speaking to Danielle Stokes?'

My husband frowns in thought and reaches out to touch my arm again.

'Danielle who?' He raises his brows, but then his

breath catches in his throat. 'Hang on, I've heard that name before. You mean... that girl that was murdered?' After a moment, he draws his head back and drops his hand from my arm. 'Why on earth would I have ever spoken to that girl?' He shakes his head, his cheeks flushing pink. 'Who have you been talking to?'

I back away. Right now, I trust Harley, a teenage boy who I barely know, more than I trust my own husband. Because Harley had hard proof on his phone.

'What were all those notifications popping up on your phone all the time? These past few months... the disappearing off into the garage to talk to someone. Coming home from work late. This all started a few months ago. And yet you've never given me an explanation for it. Just that it's a work thing and that it'll never happen again.'

Edward walks towards me and my heart pounds. I continue taking backward steps towards the front door.

'I've never seen or spoken to that girl in my entire life,' says Edward, looking at me like I'm deranged. 'The first time I ever heard her name was on the news.'

'Are you MrSugarDaddy111?'

'What even is that?' Edward says, screwing his face into an expression of disgust.

'It's a username.'

Edward pauses, then releases a short, loud laugh that sounds like a bark. 'Mr Sugar Daddy? You know me, Sara. I have no social media. I hate that crap.'

'How do I know that you haven't made secret accounts behind my back? How do I know anything about you? You don't even talk to me anymore. Unless it's about making a baby,' I say, trembling all over, my throat tight.

Outside, through the screen door, I can hear a lawnmower running. I would never have guessed that one day I'd be grateful to have a neighbour nearby because I'm feeling threatened by my own husband.

'Where has this come from? Is it because of what Stan said about Neve?' Edward asks, his voice softening. 'Sara, I've never even talked to another woman behind your back. I've never had an affair. I love you.'

Edward seems so genuine. I almost believe him, but then I remember the password he put on our shared computer.

'Why did you put a password on our computer? And it was only recent. I looked up a recipe a couple of weeks ago, without having to log on. Now there's a password on it.'

Edward's gaze flickers to the left, to where our wedding photos hang, and then to the floor.

'You've been hiding something from me,' I say, my voice breaking.

Edward's hands begin to shake, and he rakes his fingers through his hair.

When he finally meets my gaze, his eyes are brimming with tears and his entire face is red.

'Oh my God,' I say, putting my hands to my mouth, ready for my husband to confess to speaking with that dead girl.

'I've got a problem... oh God, Sara,' he murmurs, shuffling towards me, trembling all over. 'I've got a real problem. I'm... I'm addicted.'

'To... what?' I say, horrified by what he might say.

I back away again, until I'm at the screen door, and hook my fingers over the lock latch in case I need to run.

'No, no,' he says, grasping at tufts of his hair with both hands. 'Stop looking at me like that. I'm not a fucking sexual deviate,' he says, almost shouting now.

I put a hand up when he takes another step towards me.

'Don't move any closer. I don't trust you right now and I'm about to run screaming onto the street if you take another step.'

Edward swallows down his tears and puts both

hands up in surrender.

'Okay, okay. I'm going to stay right here,' he says, snorting heavily through his nostrils. 'But it's ridiculous,' he says, shaking his head. 'When you find out you'll...' He shakes his head again.

'So tell me then. What is it that I don't know? What have you been hiding from me?'

Hot blood pulses through my veins. My entire body feels so alive in this moment. The realisation that I'm not going insane. That my instincts have been right all along. That finally, after all this time, I'm going to learn the truth.

Edward looks me dead in the eye, and takes several deep breaths, before he finally speaks.

24

Sara

'I gambled away our life savings, Sara. All that money in my account. Over a million dollars. Those beeps you were hearing, those notifications blowing up my phone, they were from gambling apps.'

I say nothing in response. What Edward is saying is not what I expected.

'Every night, I've been finishing work at 5pm. But instead of going straight home, I've been going to the casino. Then when I come home, I go straight on the betting apps. I've been lying to you because I felt, no, I *feel*, so ashamed.'

'You could be making this up,' I say, after a long pause, because I've never known Edward to be a gambler in the entire time that I've been with him. He used to laugh at me whenever I would buy lotto tickets while we were dating.

'Where's the proof?' I ask, folding my arms across my chest.

Edward rubs his temple and then widens his eyes like a madman. He all but shouts Eureka.

'The beeps! They're gone because I deleted the apps. I don't have them anymore. Because after I came at you that night, you know, in bed, I felt so disgusted with myself. I was a desperate man, scared of what was coming after losing all our money, and my inheritance on top of it all after speaking to my dad – but that's no excuse for what I did. So that night, in the guest bedroom, I vowed to change. And I have, Sara. I have truly changed. I promise you.'

'Show me your banking app. I want to see the lost savings in your bank account,' I say, recalling the seven figures I saw on his bank statement not long ago.

He groans. 'Okay, okay, but before I show you, I want you to know that things have changed in the past twenty-four hours, I've been lucky and...'

'Just hand over your bloody phone.'

He nods and swipes at his phone and taps it a few times before extending his arm and handing it over, all while keeping his feet rooted to the ground.

Instead of the zero dollars I expected, I see seven digits illuminating the screen.

'Nothing's changed.' Disappointment floods my veins, making me want to cry. 'You have over a million dollars in there,' I say, confused, the pulse in my ears deafening. 'I thought you said you'd gambled away our life savings?'

He closes his eyes and breathes in deeply through his nostrils.

'Because I have money now. I know this sounds unbelievable, but I got it last night. I got the money back.'

'You *got* a million dollars last night? Just like that? Seriously? So are you saying that you gambled again? And happened to win back the money you lost? It sounds ridiculously far-fetched and a bit backwards seeing as you said you made a decision to change while in the guest bedroom.'

'It's not like that,' he says, sounding as frustrated and exhausted as I feel. 'I didn't gamble. It wasn't a win.'

'Then tell me what it's like. Tell me the truth, because I'm so sick of not knowing.'

He sighs and drops his shoulders, looking like a defeated man. 'The truth is… someone helped me out. But I can't tell you who, because I made a promise to this person.'

'Wait, did your dad help you out?'

Edward frowns. 'No. What? No way. My dad wants to disinherit me. Of course he didn't help me. I haven't spoken to Dad since the weekend. But I plan on seeing both my parents asap.'

'Then tell me who helped you?'

Edward shakes his head. 'No. I can't go back on my word. I made a promise and I stand by it.'

I flick the latch and open the door. I'm grateful now that I already have my handbag and phone with me from when I intended to buy ingredients for my celebration lasagne.

'Tell me the truth, Edward. Tell me now or I'm gone. I'll go stay with my mum and we will be over.'

Edward gasps and reaches for me.

'Sara,' he groans, burying his face into my hair. He leans against me, and I nearly lose my footing against the open screen door as it bangs against the outer brick wall of our home. 'I'm so sorry. I've made a mess of everything. I shouldn't have said yes to him. I should never...'

'Who?' I press my palms against his chest, trying to push him away from me. 'Edward, please, you need to tell me the truth.'

'I can't,' he says, lifting his head and looking me in the eye, his gaze filled with sorrow. 'You don't understand.'

The sound of a car slowing in front of our house distracts Edward and I follow his gaze as he watches the blue and white car pull into our driveway.

My breath catches in my throat.

'You called the police?' Edward asks, taking a step back, his eyes wide. 'You actually thought I had something to do with that dead girl? What on earth made you think that?'

'I didn't call them,' I say, my heart in my throat as I watch the officers step out of the vehicle.

I think about Harley. It hasn't been an hour. He must have gone straight to the police instead of waiting on me. Maybe he was scared Edward would react in anger when I told him. He may have been worried for my safety which is understandable – the boy thinks that my husband may be responsible for what happened to his sister.

'Bloody hell, Sara, you're my wife. How could you?'

'I didn't call them,' I say again.

Edward stands in the doorway, trembling.

I grab his arm. 'Eddie, look me in the eye,' I say firmly and a little gruffly.

He does.

'Listen to me. If you didn't have anything to do with this girl, with Danielle Stokes, then you have nothing to worry about.'

Edward takes a deep breath and nods.

'You're right. I didn't do anything. I just need to stay strong,' he says, nodding his head.

'That's right,' I say, gripping his arm, offering him as

much support as I can muster. 'You just need to be honest. That's all it takes. Honesty solves everything.'

He nods, makes a show of standing tall, but his hands are shaking, and I can tell that he is frightened.

Together we watch from the open doorway, as two police officers march towards us.

'Honesty solves everything,' Edward whispers to himself, echoing my words.

25

Sara

The police have taken my husband in for questioning and I'm losing my mind while I wait at home.

After two hours, I can't take it anymore, so I grab my keys, phone and handbag and drive straight to Neve and Stan's.

Both cars are in the open garage and for that I'm glad. I want to look them both in the eye and ask them what they know. If there's anything they can tell me about Edward that I'm unaware of.

Is my husband a sugar daddy? Has he been living a secret life? Is Edward capable of murder?

I shake my head at that last thought. No. Innocent until proven guilty. Just because my husband's face is on that profile doesn't mean that it's him. Anyone can get a hold of a stranger's photo these days and use it to catfish innocent victims. You read about these stories on the internet all the time.

I knock on the door, my heart racing. The longer they keep Edward at the station the more panicked I grow. Should I call his parents? His work? What do wives normally do when their husbands get taken away by the police for questioning?

The door swings open.

'Sara?' Stan says, unlocking the screen door and holding it open. 'Oh... did you say you were coming over?'

'No.' My throat tightens, and I take a deep breath. 'Is Neve home? I need to speak to you both. It's important.'

Stan closes and locks both doors once I step inside, which I find odd. It makes me feel trapped and uncomfortable.

'There have been some break-ins in the area,' he says, by way of explanation, before he sighs.

'Oh, that's not good.' I glance around their immaculate home. 'Where's Neve?'

'Unfortunately, Neve's not here. As in, not in Western Australia.'

I look at Stan, waiting for an explanation.

'Melbourne,' he says. 'She's gone to see Liv.' His cheeks tint pink as though he's embarrassed by the fact. 'It was all rather rushed. She didn't have time to message you, but she said she would when she got there.'

'Okay,' I say, frowning in confusion. 'But she only just changed her meds. Should she really be travelling on her own?'

Stan sighs and holds his hands out in front of him. 'Once Neve's got her heart set on something it's almost impossible to change her mind.'

I say nothing. Neve is probably one of the most agreeable people I've ever met. There's something not right going on here.

Now I want to leave. It feels awkward to be in Neve's house, alone with Stan. Neve's always here whenever I see him. And with what just happened with Edward, I'm not sure of who I can trust.

'So,' he says, rubbing his hands together and then gesturing to the nearby living room. 'Take a seat. Tell me what this is all about.'

I force myself to step into the living room and take a seat on the edge of the closest couch to the entrance, a plush beige two-seater. Stan remains standing. It's rather intimidating.

'The police came for Edward just now. They've taken him in for questioning.'

Stan raises his brows and after a few seconds, his face visibly pales.

'What for?' he asks, his voice hitching a little. He most certainly knows something.

'I think it's to do with the young woman. The one who was found down the street from here. Danielle Stokes.'

Stan shakes his head and then turns away. He walks over to the open window and stares out into the front garden.

'Do you know anything about this?' I ask.

Stan turns around. 'No, Sara. I know nothing. But, as I've said before, I have noticed that Edward hasn't been right lately. His dad has been calling me for months now, asking me to keep an eye on him, but you know how Eddie is.'

A silence descends between us. I knew that Stan threatened Edward with calling his father the other day, but I had no idea that Jeoffrey was already keeping tabs on Edward via Stan.

'He's been quite closed off to me too,' I say. 'But he told me, he told me that he's been gambling and that someone helped him out with his debt last night.'

Stan reels back. He seems genuinely shocked at the idea of his best friend being a gambler. 'Gambling? Eddie? That doesn't sound like him.'

'So it wasn't you that helped him out with a million dollars last night?'

Stan shakes his head. 'What? A million dollars? Are you crazy? Most of my money is tied up in the charity fund. I can't touch that money. It's against the law.' He whistles and rubs at his chin. 'I'd have to sell my house to get that kind of money. But of course, if I had it, I would absolutely have helped him. He's my best friend.'

I look Stan in the eye and wonder if he's telling the truth. His parents are loaded, much like Edward's family. They buy their children investment properties for Christmas gifts, first-class flights for stocking stuffers.

Stan finally sits down on the opposite couch.

'Eddie gambling?' He shakes his head and meets my gaze. 'Honestly I just can't see it.'

'Then what do you think he's been hiding if it's not gambling?' I ask.

Stan blushes again and shakes his head.

'You're going to think I'm an idiot,' he says, gazing over at me sheepishly. 'But I still think he may have had an affair with Neve. Even though both have denied it.' He shrugs. 'Neve never wants sex and Eddie's been avoiding me.' He raises his brows. 'So maybe they've both been screwing us over.'

I shake my head. 'No. Neve wouldn't do that to me. She's my best friend.' Nothing Stan says is ever going to convince me that Neve would see my husband behind my back.

Stan releases a long, whistling sigh, as though he read my mind and has given up trying the Edward and Neve angle. 'I need a drink. You want one? Wine? Something a little stronger?'

My body stiffens at the suggestion.

'No. Thank you. I was just leaving,' I say, getting up from the couch and heading to the front door. Stan follows me and the fact that he's behind me right now gives me goosebumps.

I do not trust this man.

I'm not sure who I can trust right now.

At that moment, my phone pings with a message.

'Excuse me,' I say to Stan while I check my phone. It's a text.

> *Love, it's me, Mum. This is my new number. Call me when you get it xx*

And just like that, I've found the one person that I can trust.

> *Thanks, Mum. Call you in a few minutes xx*

26

Sara

'Can I come get you, Mum?' I ask over the phone, my voice tight. 'I need you to come and stay over with me again. Something's happened with Edward. The police took him.'

I'm sitting in my car, which is idling in Stan and Neve's driveway, watching the curtains twitch. Is Stan in there trying to call or text Edward? Do they have something they're hiding between them?

'Of course. I can pack for a week if you like,' says Mum. 'But I can stay longer, however long you need me for.'

The relief makes my body sag against the seat.

'Yes. Thank you.'

'No worries. You head on over and I'll get ready and packed in the meantime. See you in around an hour.'

'Yep. I'll see you soon.'

I reverse out the driveway and see the curtain drop back in its place. A shiver snakes its way through my body. Something about Stan is off. He's keeping things from me. He knows more about Edward than he's saying.

Maybe, after Mum and I get home, I'll get on the phone and speak to Edith and Jeoffrey. If I tell them that Edward has been taken away for questioning by the police, then they might take the matter seriously and help us. Jeoffrey had that private chat with Edward. He must know something. Whatever they know could either help my husband, or at least help me understand what is going on.

As I put my car into drive, the lady from across the street with her oversized sunglasses that make her look like a bug grins my way.

I put my foot on the brake and slide my window down.

The woman looks at me and laughs.

'Is there something I should know?' I ask, my voice coming out harsher than I intended.

She shakes her head.

'You think you know your friend, don't you?' she says in a sing-song voice.

The sound of a lawnmowing starts up somewhere down the street.

'Of course I do. Is there something you're trying to tell me?' I ask, unable to mask the irritation in my voice.

This woman's wide grin is beyond annoying. Neve has never liked this neighbour of hers – Sondra I think her name is – and I'm starting to understand why.

'That man is a saint for staying with that woman,' she

says, her face turning serious. 'I mean, who could do that to their husband?'

'You mean Stan?'

The woman raises a single brow which rises above the frame of her sunnies.

'No, I mean the gentleman down the street. Of course I mean Stan.' She shakes her head, gets her mail out of the mailbox and turns to disappear inside her monstrous house, leaving me to wonder what on earth she meant.

While I'm stationary, I tap out a quick text to Neve.

> *Call me as soon as you can. Just want to make sure you're okay xx*

As I drive to my mother's house, I soon forget about Stan and Neve and my mind replays the conversation I had with Harley over, and over again.

You hear of stories like this, of husbands, or wives, living double lives. Unlikely people. People you would least expect.

But a sugar daddy?

Edward did save me from a life on the street, and gave me a safe home to live in. But that was done out of love, not something ego-driven to give him a sense of power.

Or was it? a voice pipes up in the back of my mind.

Laughter bubbles up my throat, even though none of this is a laughing matter. It's nervous laughter. This is ludicrous.

The truth is I'm scared. Scared that Edward is @MrSugarDaddy111 and that I've never known my husband at all. I'm scared for kids like Harley, scared for young women like his sister, Danielle, who died at the hands of another. Scared for Liv. And scared for Neve, too.

An hour later, as I pull into my mother's apartment complex carpark, my phone pings with a message.

It's from Neve.

I'm trying to find Liv.
We lied.
I don't know where my daughter is. We haven't heard from her since she left. It was after a big argument she and I had. I didn't know I'd make her leave. I didn't know my words would hurt.
But I do know that I failed her.
And it's my duty as her mother to find her. It's my fault she's gone. Because she wasn't happy with some of the choices I made.
Stan's devastated. He's been devastated all along. He wanted to come search for her, but I wouldn't let him. He's such a good man for putting up with my mistakes.
It's my job to fix this.
I'll keep you posted xx

27

Sara

Since lasagne is one hundred percent off the menu, I allow Mum to take over at the grocery store we've pulled into. My appetite has vanished, and my thoughts are completely removed from dinner, but my mother wants to make sure that I'm well fed, as mothers do.

I am of no use, walking up and down the aisles in a daze, fretting over where Liv is, worried about Neve's state of mind, and of course worrying about Edward being taken away by the police, replaying the moment of him getting into the police vehicle over and over inside my head, while Mum selects what she needs for tonight.

We arrive home with lamb chops to grill, potatoes to mash, and a garden salad to dress. Mum gets to work in the kitchen, insisting that I sit and watch while I sip from the cup of camomile tea she's brewed for me.

It's nice being taken care of, to sit and collect my thoughts.

By the time the house is filled with the aroma of rosemary-scented lamb, and I've drunk my tea, the police deposit my husband on our doorstep.

'Edward?' I call out when I hear the front door being opened.

We meet in the hallway.

Though he still looks a broken man, there's something in his eyes that gives me hope.

Relief. Edward looks relieved.

'What happened?' I ask, closing the distance between us. 'Mum's here,' I say, lowering my voice. 'She's in the kitchen looking after dinner. Let's talk in here first.'

I lead him into the living room and sit him down on the couch. Edward's face is as pale as the walls, but he holds my gaze longer than he's held it in months.

'They asked me all sorts of sick questions,' he says, clenching and unclenching his hands into fists. 'They thought I killed that poor girl.'

'That must have been awful,' I say. 'But they released you. Which means...'

'I'm not the killer. Of course I'm not,' he says, throwing me a look of hurt. 'I had an alibi. They had

CCTV footage of me. Of where I was the night the girl was killed.'

Edward closes his eyes and tilts his head to the ceiling as though in prayer.

'It's okay. You can tell me,' I say. Because anything is better than murder. Edward may be having an affair, or whatever it is. But at least he didn't murder an innocent young woman.

Edward sighs. 'I was at the casino. It was the night I lost everything. I'm on the video for the entire window of time that girl was killed.'

'Oh, Eddie, oh thank God,' I say, my body sagging with relief that my husband is a gambler, not a murderer. I touch Edward's arm, but he stiffens and moves his arm out of reach.

'But you didn't believe me when I told you that I'd gambled away our savings. That I have a problem. An addiction. You just chose to believe the worst of me.'

I sit up straighter. 'I can understand that you're upset, but... you showed me your phone. You had over a million in your bank account. Right after you said you'd lost everything, you still had money. A lot of money. And admit it, you haven't been honest with me for a while, and it's hard to believe someone who's being dishonest all the time.'

He rubs his forehead. 'Okay, okay. I'm sorry. I should have been upfront from the beginning.'

'Yeah, you should have. Because when I saw your photo on that profile...'

'How did you find out about that, anyway?' Edward asks. 'That fake account, pretending to be me?'

'The dead girl's brother showed up on our doorstep. He recognised you.'

When Edward gives me a blank stare I explain.

'Harley washes windows at the traffic lights near the petrol station.'

'That long-haired kid?' Edward snorts in disbelief.

'That's Danielle Stokes' brother?'

'Yeah. He's a good kid. Anyway, he saw that she'd been talking to this… this person behind the account, who happens to be using your photo as their profile. He followed me home one day because he saw you in my car one time, and he wanted to see if it was you.'

'Oh, okay. So I can understand you jumping to conclusions after seeing that.'

'Did the police show it to you?'

'Yeah.' He raises his brows and rubs his face. 'The fact someone is pretending to be me, writing God knows what and doing God knows what.' He shudders. 'I saw some of the stuff he'd sent that girl. All that "daddy" crap. It makes me feel sick. The police were still giving me looks, even after I was cleared.'

I shiver. 'Can they trace whoever is doing this?'

'I don't know. They wouldn't answer any of my questions about it, they just wanted information from me. It makes sense. They can't go around spilling details of an unsolved murder case.'

He reaches for my hand, and I meet him halfway, grasping his cold fingers in mine. I feel like hugging him, kissing him, despite finding out that he's a gambler who recently lost our savings. But at least he's not a murderer. I cannot believe that for a while there I doubted him, my own husband.

'We can move forward from this, Eddie,' I say. 'Let's just promise to be honest with each other from now on.'

Edward nods. 'Honesty,' he says, looking me in the eye. 'Honesty from now on,' he says, as though he's giving himself a pep talk out loud.

'So,' I say, careful to keep any tones of accusation out of my voice, 'if you did gamble our money away, then where did that million actually come from? The truth this time, please.'

Edward rubs his face. It's clear he's struggling with this honesty thing.

'I promise that I won't get upset, not matter what.'

He sighs and looks me in the eye.

'Okay. It was Stan. I ran into him while I was away. He was staying at the same hotel as me, for work.' Edward's eyes skip away from mine for just a second. But it's enough to send my bullshit detector pinging again.

'Stan? So you just happened to run into your best friend at a random hotel, and then he handed you over a million dollars just like that?' I try my hardest to keep my voice calm while I recall what Stan had said about having to sell his house if he wanted to come up with money like that. Why did Stan lie to me? Had he promised Edward that he wouldn't tell me?

I get up and stand by the window and watch the street turn golden beneath the colours of the afternoon sun. The world outside our house looks so perfect.

'I know how it sounds. It sounds crazy. But I was contemplating suicide, to be honest. My dad wouldn't help me. My mum wasn't home so she couldn't help. I felt so shitty and depressed sitting in my sterile hotel room after how I'd treated you.' He clears his throat. 'I chose a mid-range hotel because, well, I didn't feel like I deserved luxury at that point, and it wasn't like I had the money to splurge. But anyway, out of nowhere I heard a familiar voice in the hallway, so I step out of my room and it's Stan and he...'

I turn and meet my husband's gaze. He gives me a knowing look.

'He was with someone, wasn't he?' I ask.

Edward nods. 'Yes. He was there for some work conference to do with his charity. He was with a young woman. He said she works in his office. They were only talking, but they were about to enter the hotel room, so I guess that part wasn't work-related.'

'So you think Stan sleeps around behind Neve's back?'

Edward holds his hands up. 'I'm not saying anything like that.'

'Unbelievable,' I say, thinking about how much of a hypocrite Stan is, going around accusing Neve of having affairs.

I remember Neve's message.

'Neve wrote. She's in Melbourne, looking for Liv.'

'What?' Edward seems genuinely surprised. 'I thought they knew where she was. They spoke to her last week.'

My heart starts to pound. The more I think about Liv, the more I know in my gut that something is seriously wrong.

'They lied to us. Neve said so in her message. They haven't heard from her since she left home.' My stomach swirls as I look my husband in the eye. 'I've got a real bad feeling about this.'

Edward swallows thickly and rakes a hand through his hair.

'I hate to say it, but me too.'

28

Edward

I've decided to give the money back to Stan. The whole lot.

What was I thinking accepting it just like that?

To be honest, I wanted to run from Stan when first I saw him at the hotel with that young woman. Just seeing him made me feel sick to my stomach. Not because of who he was with, but because he saw me at my lowest.

However, I was a desperate man in need of salvation. A way out. So I didn't run. And after a two-minute conversation in my room, while Stan's mystery woman waited for him in his suite, Stan quickly offered to save me. Just like that.

A cool million. Transferred over to my account by the morning.

Stan's parents give money to their 'good' son freely. Because of their great disappointment in Lawrence, the dark sheep of the family, they've practically smothered Stan in their pride and wealth. It's been this way for years, and that night, I thanked my lucky stars for my spoilt best friend.

But it came at a price.

Stan made me promise not to breathe a word to anyone about our interaction. Not Sara, not Neve, not a soul.

Well, I've broken that promise now... at least, in part,

so my word is no longer good. Therefore, sending Stan his money back is the right thing to do.

Sara supports my decision. She said she is going to stand by my side and together we are going to work towards building our savings again. We are even getting a joint account, so that we can both keep on top of things money-wise.

God, I love Sara. I'm not sure what I'd do if I didn't have her support. And it makes me feel all the more guilty for the things that I've done.

Not being able to have kids has been a massive roadblock right in the middle of our marriage journey. I guess my addiction was a detour away from that roadblock. It gave me something else to think about, something else to obsess over while deep down I grieved the loss of the kids that we'd never have.

Honestly, when Sara and I took our wedding vows, I never would have imagined how difficult the road to parenthood could be. It was automatically assumed that kids would come easily to us, and that it was a matter of us deciding how many we'd like to have. We had the audacity to assume that nature would be kind to us and grant us our wishes like a genie from a lamp. We thought having children was our automatic right.

Not so, as we found out. The hard way.

But the past twenty-four hours has taught me a lot. It's taught me to be a realist and to get out of the fantasies in my head. And it's also taught me that I need to stand up for my wife.

Which is why, right this minute, I'm on the road to see my parents.

I need to see my dad and let him know that, while I acknowledge the fact that he desires grandkids, no amount of blackmailing me for the inheritance will make it happen. Nature has said no.

Anyway, Sara and I don't need the inheritance. We've got each other.

Just before I left, Sara talked about us perhaps adopting a child down the track. Though I'm not crazy about the idea, I may consider it in the future. But not right now. I've got to sort my head out first. Battle my addictions and inner demons. I'm not exactly the family kind of man at the moment. Even though it's something I always wanted as a kid.

When I was six years old in primary school, the teacher asked us to each stand up in turn and tell the class what we'd like to be when we grew up. Most of the kids said pilot, fireman, policeman, teacher, the usuals. One little girl said she wanted to be a fairy godmother, and some other kid a dragon.

But me, I said I wanted to get married and be a dad.

Most of the kids laughed at me, the teacher had a bit of a giggle too. Then she got serious and asked me the question again.

'This time, Eddie, a proper answer.' As though fairy godmother and dragon were realistic career choices.

At the time I was confused by all the laughter, and by my teacher's words, because I thought it was a proper answer.

Anyway, to shut everyone up, I said I wanted to be a rich man like my father.

My teacher's eyebrow shot up at that, and she pursed her lips, but she simply asked me to sit back down and said no more. Apparently, the desire to be rich was, in her eyes, more acceptable than the desire to be a father.

As I leave the suburbs behind and enter the greener pastures of the rural countryside, a realisation seizes hold of me.

I'm not that little kid anymore. I've deviated too far off the track of that little kid's dreams.

But I'm going to rectify that. Make some big changes. Steer myself back on track.

By the end of the day, when I arrange with my bank

for the money to be returned to Stan, I'll be a penniless man. But I'll still have my job at my father's company – well, at least, I hope I will after the conversation I'm going to be having with him very soon – and we'll still have our house.

And I will still have Sara.

Thank God.

And I'm happy for her to pursue whatever it is she wants. Whether she wishes to return to her old job, or study, or find a more altruistic career. She can do what she likes.

It's weird. But being taken away by the police… it's made everything about my life so much clearer. Sharper. I know what I want now.

A good life with Sara.

Maybe we'll get a dog, a golden retriever, or a chocolate lab. We can get a cat too. Sara's always wanted a cat. Hell, I'll get her ten cats if that's what she wants.

A good, stable, honest life.

No more darkness, no more lies.

I'm going to be a new man from now on.

* * *

An hour later, as I pull into my parents' driveway and punch the keycode in to open the wrought iron gates, I think about what Sara said about Neve's message, how Liv is missing, and that Neve has gone off to find her. The thought of not knowing exactly where Liv is, or if she's safe, leaves me feeling cold. And now Neve's gone, too. Because we have no idea where she is exactly either.

Liv is like a daughter to both Sara and me. After I've spoken to my mother and father, I plan on paying Stan a visit and asking him what on earth is going on with his daughter.

Though I'm fully psyched for what I'm about to do,

coming clean to my parents and standing up to my father about our decision to not pursue biological children anymore, my stomach still churns with apprehension while I wait on their front porch after I've knocked on the large double doors of my childhood home.

I didn't tell them I'm coming, which I know will annoy the heck out of my dad. He's an appointments man. Even with his own flesh and blood. Who knows, he might even send me away when he sees me.

But it's Mum who answers the door, her face breaking into a wide smile when she sees me through the small crack she's opened.

'Mum,' I say, smiling back. But I quickly lose my smile when she opens the door wide, and I notice how thin her arms are. She's wearing a nightie, which is unusual for Mum so late in the day. And she has something on the left side of her chest.

'What's this, Mum?'

Mum's wrinkled hands flutter to cover the bandages below her collarbone.

'Oh, it's nothing. Just a little medical procedure.'

But it dawns on me what it is. One of my colleagues, she had cancer a couple of years ago and the doctors installed a port in her chest, for ease of administering chemotherapy treatment and for taking blood samples.

'Why didn't you tell me and Sara about this last weekend?'

Tears fill her eyes, and she tries to speak but the words don't come.

'It's okay, Mum,' I say, stepping inside and wrapping my arms around her gently. She feels so fragile, no bigger than a small child. How did I not notice this last weekend? Why didn't I think it strange that she was wearing that oversized tracksuit, even when it was warm enough for short sleeves in the afternoon sun?

Emotions tighten my chest and thicken my throat.

And all along I was thinking that my dad may have been sick, with his heart. That's why I thought he gave me the ultimatum about the inheritance.

'I'm sorry, Eddie,' she croaks.

'Don't be,' I say, stroking her hair, which has thinned. Again, how did I not notice this? Was I so wrapped up in my own shitty problems that I didn't notice my mother's illness?

'I didn't want you to know. I made your father promise not to tell you.'

At the mention of my father I can't help but stiffen and draw back.

'Where is Dad? I need to have a word with him. With you both,' I say firmly.

'Please don't be mad at him,' Mum says, her green eyes wide. 'I made him promise not to tell you.'

I shake my head. Why is she always defending him?

'Dad,' I call out, my booming voice echoing down the grand hallway. Now I'm angry. Angry that I wasn't told something so important as my own mother becoming sick.

But there was no need to shout, because my father is walking towards us already, his face blank, unreadable.

'Why didn't you tell me?' I say, my voice breaking, even though I'm yelling. 'You were so busy threatening me with my inheritance. How could you let me drive away not knowing that Mum was sick?' I can feel my blood pressure rising, the blood boiling in my veins, burning me up from inside out. 'How could you be so selfish?'

Dad comes to stand by my mother's side and sighs deeply, as though he's dog-tired and doesn't have the energy for this discussion. When he looks at me, his shoulders sink. If there was any fight in him a second ago, it's gone now.

'It wasn't my place to tell,' he says, his voice soft, his gaze gently resting on Mum. Then he adds, palms raised,

'This is... nobody's fault. This is just...' – he shakes his head – 'nature reminding us that we're not in charge.'

'Of course it's nobody's fault,' I say to them both, feeling like an arse for having allowed my temper to get the better of me. They both look so much older now, so resigned to the fact that uncertainty lies ahead. The last thing they need is me getting on their backs simply because I wasn't told.

'What's all this about threats and the inheritance?' Mum asks, frowning in confusion. She looks weak, as though she might faint.

'Wait. Let's sit you down first, love,' says Dad, gently resting a hand on my mum's waist and guiding her into the lounge room nearby.

It's touching how gentle and protective he's being. But I'm still mad at him.

We sit on the leather couch, which gives us a magnificent view of the front rose garden and the large fountain at the centre of it all.

My mother watches as several tiny birds flit in and out of the fountain stream while my father wrings his hands, a habit I seemed to have picked up in my thirties. It's all I did at the police station while they relentlessly questioned me about Danielle Stokes.

'Your mother had nothing to do with my threat to take away your inheritance. That was my doing.' He rubs his face with both hands and suddenly he looks like an old man, his hair greyer, his wrinkles deeper. 'It's just... I wanted your mother's happiness. She's always dreamed of holding a grandchild in her arms.' He sucks in a deep breath and takes a pause, his head down. I've never seen my father cry, but this is close.

'I can speak for myself, you know,' says Mum, her pale cheeks flushed with a little bit of colour.

'I know,' Dad says, raising his head and rubbing her back. 'But I was desperate,' he continues, turning his attention to me. 'I didn't know how else to convince you to try once more. It thought that if your mother knew there was a baby on the way, she might fight a little harder and get well again.' He shakes his head. 'But it was wrong of me.' He frowns and widens his eyes in momentary horror. 'Poor Sara. I can't believe I asked you to put her life at risk again like that. I'm sorry.'

I take a moment to speak. My father has never said sorry in the entire time I've known him. And the shock of it seems to have dissolved my anger. Even Mum seems surprised at Dad's apology.

'It's okay,' I say, feeling a sudden and immense amount of compassion for him. 'I understand. You were doing it for Mum.'

Dad nods but Mum frowns.

'I think I'm partly to blame. I cried my head off like a fool last Friday, sobbing about not being around when... well, when the little ones come.' She stops and her eyes flicker from Dad to me. 'I think your father was just trying to... change my mind...' Mum's voice trails off and she shifts her gaze to the floor.

'You need to tell him, love,' says my dad, his eyes on Mum.

Mum's eyes film over with tears, and she shakes her head.

'I don't want to, Jeoffrey, and I don't have to.'

'It's okay, Mum,' I say. 'You can tell me anything.'

Mum sighs softly and her bony shoulders droop.

'I'm dying, love. It's terminal. I have a year at most.'

I take a while to respond. This can't be. I glance up at Dad and his eyes betray the composure of his face. He's terrified of losing Mum. Just as scared as I'm feeling right now. I can understand why he's aged so suddenly.

'Are you sure?' I ask, stupidly. 'Sometimes the doctors are wrong. I can make some calls. I think Sara's mum knows about some herbal stuff from when her friend had it all those years ago.' I take Mum's hand in mine. 'There's a lot we can do, Mum. We can fight this.'

Dad's sighs and gives me a look that says, *good luck*.

Mum kisses my hand. Both are staring at me like I'm some creature to be pitied.

'Next week is the last chemo I'll receive. I've decided that I don't want any more treatment. It's only prolonging the inevitable. I want to enjoy the last year of my life,' she says, smiling.

The leather couch squeaks as my mother shifts closer to my father. He puts an arm around her and smiles down at her tenderly.

'We're going to travel, darling,' says my mother. 'Visit some of my favourite places. I want to be around nature. Witness some magical sunsets.'

'I respect your right to a choice, Mum, but...'

My father shakes his head at me, and I swallow down my protests and nod.

'Okay, okay,' I say, my voice hoarse.

'We want you to join us on some of the trips. You and Sara. It would be wonderful to have you both with us, our family all together,' Mum says.

I blink and focus on the way the afternoon sun turns the fountain sprays to glitter. A life without Mum. It's an unbearable thought.

'Now, Eddie, what was it that you wanted to talk to us about?'

I sigh. The last thing I want to do is give my parents something extra to worry about, but I feel I owe my parents some honesty, considering how hard it must have been for Mum to speak up about her terminal illness.

'Well,' I say, wringing my hands together. 'I've gotten myself into a bit of trouble lately. I've been gambling. I lost a million dollars. Everything Sara and I have worked hard for, and the money you both gave us to help with the house. All gone.'

There. I said it.

Dad's face drops, but he doesn't look particularly

surprised. Though my mother's loving expression betrays nothing, I can feel the disappointment radiating off them both.

'But I've given up,' I say, holding my palms up. 'I've made a promise to Sara. It's not going to be easy. But I'm going to work extra hard for your company, Dad, and get all that money back. And I think, without all the stress of worrying about pregnancies and Sara's future health, I probably won't even feel the need to gamble anymore. Gambling was an escape. But...' I shrug. 'I don't need that anymore. Not after I've faced up to the truth' – I pause and clear my throat after my voice breaks – 'that we can never have children.'

Mum closes her eyes for a long time, as though she's drifted off to sleep, and then she opens them again.

'Oh, Eddie,' she says, tears shining in her eyes. 'It's okay, love.'

Dad looks at me, brows raised. 'We can help. Replace the money you lost.'

I shake my head. 'No, Dad. Thanks. But no. The best way for me to learn is to earn it all back myself.'

Dad's face brightens and he gives me a smile I haven't seen since I was a little boy. It is what makes me decide, then and there, not to tell them about the police and the fact that I was dragged in for questioning relating to a murder. It'll be too much for them. They don't deserve that kind of stress.

'You'll beat this, Edward. I can tell,' says Dad.

'Why are you both being so good about this?' I ask, still mildly suspicious at how well they're taking it all.

Dad sighs. 'Stan has been calling me. He told me he was worried about you. That he thought you were hiding something, maybe having an affair behind Sara's back.' He shrugs. 'It's another reason why I threatened the inheritance. I thought that if I forced you back to Sara, you might forget about whoever it was that you were seeing.'

'Stan said this?' I look at them both. 'You know it's ridiculous, right? I'd never do that to Sara.'

Dad nods. 'You're right. And now that I know you've been hiding a gambling problem, I can see how ridiculous Stan's suggestion was. Of course you wouldn't do that to Sara. At heart, you're a good man, Eddie. A great man. And I'm proud of you. We both are.'

I can't believe the words coming out of my father's mouth. But I can't deny that they make me feel good. Like a worthy son.

Mum reaches for my hand, and I shuffle in closer.

'There. Now. We're a family again. I think this celebratory moment calls for some bubbly.'

'Mum, should you be drinking?'

Mum gives me a look, and my father and I hide shared grins.

'Okay, okay,' I say, palms up. 'I'll go get us a bottle and some flutes.'

'That's better,' Mum says, a soft smile on her lips and a bit of sparkle back in her eyes. She reaches for my other hand and breathes in deep, closing her eyes briefly. 'Doesn't it feel wonderful to get things off your chest, Eddie? I feel so much better already, don't you?'

'Yeah, I do,' I say, but as I head into the kitchen, my smile drops away. Because I haven't been entirely honest.

If I was, then I'd be heading straight back to the police station this minute.

29

Sara

While Mum is napping in the guest bedroom, I get on my laptop and begin searching counselling courses in the kitchen.

I'm so absorbed in reading up on a youth counselling certificate that I'm interested in studying, that I jump when I hear the screen door slam, heralding Edward's return.

I lean back on my seat and stare down the hallway, catching sight of the apricot-pinkish sky through the door.

It's later than I thought. I should have woken my mother over an hour ago. Now she won't sleep a wink tonight, all because I got too distracted on my computer.

'Hey,' he says, tossing his keys onto the counter and rubbing his face with both hands. 'How has your afternoon been?'

'Okay,' I say. 'Mum's been a great distraction, but my head is still filled with, well, everything, especially Liv and Neve. I'm really worried now.'

'Me too,' he says, his eyes on the counter but his mind elsewhere.

'I keep reading over Neve's message and the more I look at it the more I read into it. What does Neve mean about failing as a mother? Why would she write that? And... I don't like that they lied about having heard from her when they hadn't. Why would they do that? It's almost as though they're hiding something from us.' I shake my head. 'And how does Neve know Liv's in Melbourne if they haven't heard from her?'

My husband nods but continues to stare into space.

'Eddie, are you okay? How did it go with your parents?'

He blinks and stares at me for a long time before he says, 'Mum has cancer, Sars. She's dying.'

It takes me about half a minute to process those last two words.

'What? Oh my God,' I say, nearly slipping off my stool. I think back to the weekend. Of how Edith had shouted at me to get out of the bathroom. Poor Edith. She mustn't have wanted me to see her. She'd obviously worked hard on trying to shield Edward and me from the news. I shake my head and watch my husband try to hold it together. 'I can't believe it. I'm so sorry.'

'Yeah,' he says, his voice tight. 'She has about a year. She wants us to all go travelling together… make the most of the time she has left.'

I get up from my stool and slip my arms around Edward. 'Oh no, Eddie. This is just awful. How long has she known?'

'I'm not sure. But she's already had chemo. So she's likely known for a while. Dad knew as well of course.'

'And he still blackmailed you for a baby?'

Edward's shoulders sag and I stand back and listen to what he has to say, my arms folded across my chest.

'Well, it turns out he was doing it for Mum. She sobbed the day before we came, about how she's going to miss out on holding her future grandchildren.' Edward sighs. 'Dad said he was desperate for Mum to find something to cling to, something to live for. Because she's decided to give up chemo. She wants to live out the rest of her time without treatment.' Edward looks me in the eye, his gaze filled with sadness. 'Dad's sorry though, really sorry to have even suggested putting you through that again.'

I'm not sure what to say. Edith has always been so wonderful, so welcoming. A year? How can that be possible? She's only sixty-three years of age. And yes, despite it not being my fault, it hurts that she won't get to hold a grandchild.

'Well, we'll just have to grant your mum her other wish. Wherever she wants to travel, we'll go along with her and be right by her side. Your dad too,' I say, my voice croaky. I sniff as the reality hits. 'He's going to be so lost without her. They really do everything together, don't they?'

'Yeah,' says Edward, releasing me and moving to the other side of the breakfast bar.

'We should go visit them this weekend,' I suggest. 'Help them out in whatever way we can. We can plan a magical trip together. I think that will give everyone a nice little boost, something good to think about and look forward to.'

Edward takes a glass out of the cupboard and pours himself some water from the tap. I haven't noticed until now that he's sweating at his temples.

'Maybe you should have a shower,' I say, remembering Mum. 'I'll go wake Mum up. Can't believe I've let her sleep this long.' I smile in an attempt at lightening the mood.

Edward chugs down the entire glass of water and sets the tumbler in the sink.

'I can't stay. I'm going out,' he says, forcing a casual air into his voice.

'Wait. You've only just gotten home, and we still have so much to talk about.'

'That can wait,' he says, picking up his keys again. 'This is important.'

The hairs on the back of my neck prickle. This reminds me of Edward pre-today's bombshells, the

Edward who hid things from me, like his gambling.

'Can it wait until tomorrow?'

Edward stiffens and his face reddens.

'It's important,' he says, unable to meet my eyes. 'I'll be a couple of hours max. I can't tell you about it now, but I will once I have more answers.'

'What does that even mean?' I ask, feeling the hot flush of irritation warming my blood. 'This had better not be anything to do with gambling.'

'It's not,' he says. 'You need to trust me on this.'

I say nothing, because I want to learn to trust my husband. So I simply watch him disappear out the front door.

Mum enters the kitchen, her hair matted at the back of her head. She makes herself a cup of coffee.

'Would you like one too?' she asks, as she spoons a heaped spoon of instant coffee into her favourite mug. 'It looks like you could do with a bit of a chat.'

I nod. And once I have my coffee in my hands, I tell her about Edith.

Mum is terribly saddened by the news, and after our coffees, the two of us spend some time on my laptop, searching up some holiday destinations for Edith's last wish.

'I'm going to make a start on dinner,' Mum says, while I admire pictures of the Adriatic coast.

Once Mum's busy, I close my laptop and disappear into my bedroom. The holiday destinations can wait.

Something about Edward disappearing like that is bugging me.

After I lock the bedroom door, I take out my phone and open Instagram.

The mattress squeaks as I sit down on the edge of my bed.

I hate sneaking around and doing things like this. But I need to know if my husband is hiding something. If he's living a double life.

I need to know the truth.

I need to know who is behind the Instagram account that was speaking to that poor girl before she died.

I click on 'add new account'.

My heart pounds as I type in a fake username.

@MissSugarBaby007

I fill in the rest of my details and use an email address that I still have in my maiden name from years ago.

I add a profile pic of a beautiful young actress and write what I'm looking for in the bio.

Baby looking for her Daddy...

Done.

Then I search for @MrSugarDaddy111.

My heart skips a beat when the account shows up.

How have the police not shut this down yet? But then again, why would they? It makes more sense for them to keep an eye on it.

I click on the account and my blood runs cold.

Though I've seen the profile before on Harley's phone, it's even more horrifying when I see it on my own phone.

Whoever this is has added a post since I last saw his profile. It was uploaded only one minute ago.

Edward walked out the door two minutes ago.

Did he start his car and then post this before he took off? Is this the urgent matter he is attending to?

I don't want to believe that my husband is behind this. I want nothing more than to trust Edward. But in order to do this, I need to find out who *is* behind this account.

The picture is of a pile of cash fanned out against a pillow. It's not one of our pillows, of that I'm certain. So if it is Edward, then he's used a random image from the internet. Or, and I shiver at the thought, it's a photo he's taken in some dodgy hotel room he's stayed at in the past.

> *Which little baby wants to rest her pretty head on a pillow like this...*

Though the caption churns my stomach, I open @MrSugarDaddy111's DMs and send him a message, along with a copy of the photo he posted.

> *Me xx*

30

@MrSugarDaddy111

I needed to get away. Needed time to think. This is the first time I've booked a hotel room to be alone in. To simply sit with myself and sort my head out.

I hadn't planned on getting a message from a baby during this time.

It's not like I need to get into any more trouble.

But here I am. My fingers moving over my phone as though they have no connection to my brain.

So much for time alone – time alone to figure out a way to dig myself out of the hole I'm in.

Despite being annoyed at myself, for my extreme lack of self-control, excitement zips through my veins, burning through my body like fire.

A new baby is coming to see me soon and I cannot deny that the anticipation is slowly bringing me to life. A moment ago, I felt at the depths of my despair. Paranoid. Weak. Stupid.

Now, I feel in charge again.

My tumbler is empty, so I pour myself another measure of whisky from the minibar and tell myself that this will be the last time that I do this.

My wife is becoming suspicious. She's starting to look at me strangely.

My best friend is becoming a right pain in the arse. Messaging me every second. Asking me to meet him. I think he's put two and two together. He's worked it out.

That's it, I think, as the whisky goes down my throat like fire. After tonight, no more Mr Sugar Daddy for me.

The whisky warms my belly but makes me feel melancholic.

I'll be sad to say goodbye to this. I feel like a superhero being forced to hang up my mask. Or maybe more of an anti-hero.

I open my phone and reread the messages I was sent. I'm hard by the time I get to the last one, which includes a pic of her bare breasts.

This new one seems a lot more mature. Wiser. She was reluctant to send the picture at first, but eventually relented.

They all do if you push them enough. Or ignore them.

It's a blurry pic, but enough to get me going.

@MissSugarBaby007

Her username makes me smile.

I can already tell by the way she texts that this will be a feisty one.

Which is a bit of a risk, truth be told. Feisty women do not like to be controlled.

But it's a risk that I'm willing to take for my last hurrah.

It'll make her eventual compliance even sweeter, I think, as I study the blurry image.

And after tonight, once my alter-ego is gone, I'll go back to being a good man.

And I'll forget everything that I've done.

Because it won't have been me, the good man, who killed that unfortunate girl.

It will have been @MrSugarDaddy111 who did it.

And after tonight, that man will no longer exist.

31

Sara

Although I was told by @MrSugarDaddy111 to wear something sexy, along with an apology for not having arranged a dress for me to wear – tonight was last-minute for him, apparently – I choose to wear a pair of practical black leggings, a crème shirt, and a chocolate-brown cardigan. Something comfortable that will allow me to run should I need to.

Anyway, the sexy clothes won't be necessary once I enter his room. Because he's going to have other things to worry about besides sex.

My plan is to confront him and to get a photo of his true identity, then run out of the room, screaming bloody murder if necessary.

I'll call my mum before I go in. As a security blanket. I won't say where I am or what I'm doing. But at least the police will be able to trace my last call from the hotel should something happen to me. They can do that, can't they?

I would call Edward if, well, if I didn't suspect, even just a tiny bit, that it could be him.

A cold shiver travels from my head to my toes as I brush my hair and tie it back into a neat and practical ponytail.

No. It's not going to be Edward. It can't be.

But I'm not going to just sit around while someone out there is pretending to be him.

'You can do this,' I say to myself as I coat my lips with lip balm.

'Mum,' I say, when I come into the kitchen. 'Sorry. One of the girls from work needs a chat. Relationship issues,' I say, with a shrug.

'Oh,' says Mum, her face red from being in a hot kitchen. She pokes a fork into a boiling pot and pulls out a creamy chunk of potato. 'These are done. I hope you'll be home in time for dinner. I've made so much. Will Edward be home soon?'

'Good question. I'm not sure. But he can help himself when he gets home.' I inhale. 'Gosh, it smells amazing though. Can you please save me a plate? I'll be home in an hour or so, I hope.'

Mum bangs the spoon on the rim of the saucepan and then turns off the heat and narrows her gaze at me.

'You seem to be in a hurry to get away from me.' She grabs a nearby tea towel and wipes her hands on it. 'You're not off to do something silly, are you?'

'Of course not.' I swipe my keys from the hook and take my handbag and phone. 'I won't be long.'

Mum raises her brows. 'I hope so. Drive safe.'

'I will. Bye, Mum,' I say, pecking her on the cheek, resisting the urge to hug her tight so she doesn't grow suspicious, before I rush down the hallway toward the front door.

The air is cool outside, and I shiver, despite the warmth of my cardigan, before I get into my car and start it up.

Our street is quiet. It's past 6pm and most have returned home from school or work and the houses are lit up warmly inside, the windows glowing. I want to be like these people, wrapped up in the safety of their families. But I can't really do that without the answers I need.

After I reverse out the driveway and put the car in drive, I scream and slam on the brakes as my headlights illuminate a person standing in front of me.

Harley.

I slide down my window and stick my head out.

'You scared the living crap out of me.'

He walks over to the passenger seat, looking as pale as a ghost, and gets in.

'Sorry. I didn't want to knock on your front door in case your husband answered. The police told my parents they released him. That there's video proof he couldn't have hurt my sister.'

I don't answer right away. Because I feel awful for Harley and his family. They were so close to getting answers, and now it's back to having no clue as to who took the life of their precious daughter and sister.

'It's true,' I finally say, thinking about Edward's lock-tight alibi. I mentally admonish myself for even thinking that the man I'm about to meet could be Edward. Of course @MrSugarDaddy111 is not my husband. Edward is a good man. He's made some bad choices lately. But he's not the kind of man to have an affair behind my back. Or the kind of man that hurts women.

'I still think it's that guy. The one she was talking to. Whoever it is,' Harley says, as I start driving. 'He's the murderer.'

My blood runs cold. I do not need to hear this right before I meet the guy.

'What makes you think it's him?' I ask, my voice quavering. 'It could have just been her boyfriend, the cheating one. He may have been trying to trick her by talking to her online and pretending to be another guy.'

'Flynn? No way,' says Harley. 'He was always too busy messaging other girls to bother with messaging his own girlfriend.'

We're silent for a long time.

'That's sad.'

'What?'

'That your sister, that she...'

'Had such a shit boyfriend? I know,' says Harley.

'I'm sorry,' I say. 'I shouldn't even be bringing it up.'

'It's okay.'

'So where am I taking you? Would you like to be dropped off at home?'

He shrugs. 'I might go and wash some windows. I need to help Mum and Dad so we can have a funeral for Dani. Can you drop me at the usual spot?'

'At night? No way.' I pull over and put my car into neutral and turn to face Harley. 'You don't have to work tonight. I have money. I can drive to an ATM and get you some cash. My daily limit is a grand, but I can give you more each day, until you and your family have enough to pay for your sister's funeral. That way you can give her a beautiful send-off, the kind that she deserves.'

Harley frowns and I can tell that he isn't used to accepting help. 'Why would you do that?'

I stare out the car window and watch a father and his two young daughters who are out walking a small white dog on a leash. It's a touching scene and although it's getting dark outside, I can still see the expression of joy and excitement on the girls' faces as they talk and laugh with their father.

Danielle Stokes was once like those young girls, filled with the promise of a long and exciting life ahead of her.

'Because you and your family deserve to celebrate your sister's life properly.'

He stares out the passenger window and his hands make fists. His knuckles look too big for him.

'I know it's tough to accept help,' I say. 'I've had to do it too. I know how it feels.'

'How would you know?' he says, his voice low and gruff.

'I lived on the streets many years ago,' I say, and Harley quickly turns his head to meet my gaze.

'You're rich. You've got money.'

I nod. 'But I didn't always have it. Do you want to know where I met my husband? At a soup kitchen. He was handing me my one hot meal for the day. That free soup used to be the highlight of my day.'

Harley blinks several times and swallows thickly.

'I would never have known,' he says quietly. Then he adds, 'Where did you sleep?'

'I lived in my car. But I used to go to the twenty-four-hour McDonald's on cold nights. I'd walk in with an empty coffee cup from the bin out the front so that it looked like I was a paying customer. Then I'd find a corner booth to hide away in and drift off to sleep wondering what it would be like to order a whole meal, anything I wanted from the menu. I used to torture myself with that. The pain in my empty stomach was excruciating.'

'Wow,' he says, looking at me with newfound respect in his eyes. 'So you were a street kid.'

I smile. 'I was. But I guess that part of you never leaves you. You can take the girl away from the streets, but you can never take the streets away from the girl,' I say, half-smiling.

'Yeah,' he says, smiling at my poor attempt at lightening the mood.

But his smile soon vanishes, and I wonder if he's thinking about his sister. Will he ever be able to move forward from this, from the pain, from the grief, from the feelings of outrage and injustice? I can't imagine how his parents must be feeling right now, losing their beautiful daughter like this.

'So can I help you, please? Can I drive you to the ATM?'

Harley sucks in a ragged breath and eventually sighs. 'Okay. Yes. Thank you.' He nods to a car that has slowed down across the road. 'Who's that? He's staring at us.'

I glance at the car and stiffen when I recognise the forest green vehicle. But as soon as I lock eyes with Lawrence, he puts his foot down and drives away.

'Do you know him?' Harley asks.

'No,' I lie. I'm not sure why I'm lying. But I feel a sense of duty to Harley. To protect this teenage boy from all the dark things that dwell in our world, including my inner fears. I'm not sure what I think about Lawrence being on my street, but the goosebumps rising along my arms are enough to worry me.

We're both quiet as I drive to the nearest ATM machine at the local shopping centre. Although the grocery store is still open, there are only about five cars in the carpark.

'I won't be long,' I say, taking my purse and getting out of the car.

I'm going to be late for @MrSugarDaddy111 but I don't care. Helping Harley has made me feel warm again, human.

'Here,' I say, climbing back in the car, a thousand dollars cash in hand.

But the car is empty.

I get out and glance around the near-empty carpark.

'Harley?' I call out but get nothing back.

The night is still, I can't even hear footsteps echoing down the street. All I can hear is an owl hooting somewhere in the distance.

For a second I fear that Lawrence has picked him up, but he drove off in the opposite direction and I would have noticed if he'd turned and followed us. I would have heard a car pull up. It couldn't have been him. He doesn't even know Harley.

'Harley?'

I continue to call out, and even try reasoning with him, but give up after a few minutes. He must have run home.

Oh, Harley. His pride must have gotten to him in the end.

I'll keep the money aside, tuck it in my purse for when I see him next. When he next surprises me with his presence. Or I can just look for him where he washes car windows.

Reluctantly, I put my car into gear and drive away.

Harley's no longer here to distract me from what I'm about to do. It's time I finally meet the person pretending to be my husband.

When I pull up at the hotel, the neon sign turns the inside of my car blue.

If he's a sugar daddy, then he's not exactly advertising himself well by choosing this place. It's not terrible. The rooms, I hear, are reasonable and clean – I'd certainly stay here. But it just doesn't scream sugar daddy. There are so many other, more luxurious hotels he could have chosen. Hotel Stanton is the kind of hotel you'd conduct business in at most. It's merely a place to rest your head.

Or meet someone you shouldn't be meeting.

Maybe that's the whole point. It's not the kind of establishment where Edward or anyone in his wealthy circle of friends would choose to stay.

Whoever is doing this is just acting out a fantasy, and it doesn't matter where this fantasy happens.

Here goes, I think, as I stare out my car window and mentally prepare myself for what I'm about to do.

I grab my handbag and reach for my phone, but gasp when I see that it's not in its usual place in the middle console. I check the gaps on either side of it, down the side of both seats, but it's not there.

My chest tightens in panic. I know I brought it with me.

With dread spreading through my veins, I spend an extra five minutes meticulously checking beneath and around each seat, in case it fell and slid into a narrow crevice. But no such luck.

My mobile phone is not in this vehicle.

Which can only mean one thing.

Harley took it.

I stare up at the hotel, questioning whether I'm stupid for still wanting to go through with this without the safety of my phone.

But in less than half a minute, I get out of my car, lock it and pull my handbag over my shoulder.

Now that I'm here I can't bring myself to turn around and go home never knowing who @MrSugarDaddy111 is.

I may never get this opportunity again.

Yeah, because you might die.

I tell my inner voice to shut the hell up and walk to the hotel entrance with a churning stomach and a pounding heart.

Here goes.

32

Sara

The gilded brass doors slide open as I approach the hotel entrance.

Once inside I shiver at the icy cold air conditioning. Why do all hotels do this? Create their own seasons? And it's not like I need another reason to tremble. I'm already a shaking, nervous wreck.

Despite it being dinner time, the hotel restaurant only has a handful of diners, each sitting alone at separate tables. Businesspeople. That's what this hotel is known for. It's not exactly a family hotel. And I wouldn't call it romantic either.

But then I pass bouquets of white roses and chrysanthemums and a lovely couch setting in the foyer on my way to the reception desk and eat my own words. The more I see of it, the more I realise that Hotel Stanton is quite a decent hotel – not luxurious by any means, but nice enough. It turns my stomach that @MrSugarDaddy111 uses this place for his hook-ups.

After waiting in line behind a businesswoman dressed in a killer skirt suit, I finally get seen by the receptionist.

I hadn't planned on speaking to reception. I was going to go straight up to the room number I was given. Of course, if I still had my phone I was simply going to speak to my mother for a bit, before entering the room, so that the police have enough to trace my call should I not return home tonight.

But now, without my phone, no thanks to Harley, I need to come up with another safety net.

'Hello, how may I help you?' the pretty young woman with dark bobbed hair says. Her badge tells me her name is Bethany.

'Oh, I'm meeting somebody in room 58 and I'd like to order a bottle of bubbly to be sent to the room roughly five minutes after I've gone up. Would that be possible?'

Bethany grins at me, revealing glowing white teeth.

'Of course. Is there a particular brand you'd like? I can offer you the wine list to peruse.'

'No need,' I say, thinking about whoever it is that is

up there. 'Just pick the most expensive one and charge it to the account.' That'll teach him for using my husband's photo.

Bethany hesitates. I get the feeling she is considering getting permission from the person who booked and paid for the room, and for a moment panic tightens my chest.

'Or I can pay for it right now,' I say, shrugging, acting nonchalant.

Bethany winks at me and lowers her voice. 'No need. It'll ruin the surprise. I'll send a bottle of our finest to you in roughly five minutes.'

'Exactly five minutes,' I say, grimacing a little. 'Sorry. It's just that my surprise is kind of a timed thing. And please just ask whoever brings it up to unlock the door and bring it right into the room.'

Bethany quirks an eyebrow but then her face relaxes into a smile. 'Of course. Whatever you say. Exactly five minutes,' she says. 'I finish in five, so how about I bring it up to you myself. That way I'll know it'll get done.'

'Wonderful,' I say, feeling a little disappointed that this tiny young woman with wrists the size of a five-year-old is going to be the one coming to my aid should I need it, but at least she can sound an alarm should I be in trouble, or run for help.

When I leave the reception desk, I'm trembling all over, and nearly bang into the man who is waiting in line behind me. I almost topple over.

'Sorry.'

'Not at all,' he says, smiling at me, his hand lingering on my waist for a second after he catches me.

I straighten up, hoping that I haven't just run into @MrSugarDaddy111 himself. But the man is already looking at Bethany.

'Thank you,' I say, before I head toward the elevators. My stomach is a churning sea by now and I'm relieved that the elevator is empty when the doors slide open.

As I rise toward the third level, my stomach feels as though it has fallen right out of me and is pressing against the floor of the elevator. When the doors glide open, I'm relieved to see that nobody is skulking about along the corridors.

As I near the room, I almost chicken out and step inside a door marked 'Linen'. There, I stand between piles of bedsheets and stacks of clean towels and take several deep breaths to get a hold of myself.

I need to calm down. This will all be over in a few moments. The mystery behind @MrSugarDaddy111 will be solved. I just need to get to the room, knock on the door and enter.

After some slow, deep breaths, I'm as ready as I'll ever be.

I step out of the linen cupboard and paste on a smile as a woman with closely cropped black hair walks by me.

After a few more steps along a beige-carpeted bend, there it is.

Door 58.

I knock, glad that there is no peephole on the door, and while I wait, I pray that Bethany at the reception desk is arranging my bottle of bubbly as we speak. It's already been at least three minutes, so she'll be here very soon.

The door opens enough for me to enter, but not to see who's standing behind it.

'Come in,' says a voice from the dark shadows of the room. And although there is a forced gruffness to it, I recognise it immediately.

But before I can call out his name, a hand reaches out from the darkness, roughly seizing my wrist, and yanks me inside.

33

Bethany

I get off the phone to the restaurant, having just ordered the bottle of champagne for that woman. They said they'll bring it right over to reception so that I can deliver it personally myself. I hope it comes soon. I'm dying to get out of here.

Jenny should be here by now, but there's no sign of her. Staff are supposed to come in ten minutes early for the shift changeover. It allows us to update the next rostered staff member on what's been happening and to keep up with any outstanding customer requests, such as the bottle of expensive bubbles which I can see a waiter carrying across the lobby towards the reception desk.

'Thank you so much, Dennis,' I say, smiling to the waiter. 'Just in time.'

As he walks away, I look at the time. Where the hell is Jenny?

Luckily there are no customers about, and most of the check-ins are complete for the night, save a couple who haven't arrived yet, and any potential walk-ins.

I duck out behind reception to the storeroom out the back to find a dining trolley. After I find one, I dress it up with a pretty, white cloth. I place the ice-bucket at the centre and then scatter a few handcrafted chocolates that we leave on the edge of the bed for our guests, just to make it look fancy.

By the time I roll the trolley out, Jenny still hasn't arrived.

I'm really starting to get mad, but then my stomach does a little flip when I see Rowland walk in, tucking his shirt into his pants and running his long fingers through his dark hair.

'What are you doing here?' I ask, acting annoyed when in truth, my entire body is jumping for joy and my heart is melting on the spot. I've been crushing on Rowland for the longest time. And finally, after trying to catch his eye for months, he's started to notice me. In fact, for the past week he's been very suggestive about what he'd like to do to me, and it's been driving me wild.

'Jenny called in sick. She went out last night. An all-nighter,' he says, grinning in a way that makes my stomach flutter.

'How do you know this?' I ask, trying to sound casual, when in truth I'm hoping Jenny hasn't been trying to steal Rowland away from me.

Rowland raises his brows and fixes his blue eyes on me, making my knees weak.

'Are you jealous, Beth?' he says, glancing around us to make sure that the coast is clear before he backs me through the storeroom door and presses me up against the wall. 'Jenny posted about her night out on the group chat. If you'd taken the time to read it, you would have known.'

'Well some of us have to work,' I say, sounding breathless, because I am.

'God,' he says, his voice low and ragged. 'You're so hot. I could take you right here, right now,' he says.

I can tell he means it, because I can feel him growing hard against me.

'It's a shame you're finishing now, and that we won't get to work the shift together,' he says, waggling his eyebrows suggestively.

I take a peek out at reception, over Rowland's shoulder. There's nobody about. They're either in the restaurant or up in their rooms, no doubt tapping away on their laptops.

These business types are so boring.

Not like Rowland and me.

'I can stay back. I'll lie and tell the boss we were flat out and that you needed my help.'

Rowland's lips leave a hot trail down my neck. 'Let's do it, Beth,' he whispers in my ear, his warm breath sending delicious shivers down my spine. 'I want you right now.'

He closes the storeroom door behind us, and I hear the lock click.

We're in darkness, with just a strip of light at the bottom of the door, but we don't need to see. Our hands know where to go, to all the right spots, and soon I've undone his pants and he's yanked my underwear to the side.

As the stationary shelf rattles with our movements, and my pleasure mounts, I suddenly remember the bottle of bubbly sitting out in reception, waiting to be delivered.

'Oh... fuck... oh Bethany.' Rowland's breath catches in my ear and his moans grow louder.

I shove the woman's anxious face out of my mind and run my fingernails down Rowland's back, making him moan even harder.

Surely a few more minutes won't hurt.

34

Harley

A cat passes me on the street, its eyes flashing, and I put out my hand for it to sniff. It approaches me cautiously at first, and then, after a quick smell of my fingers, allows me to pat its soft black fur.

But it darts away to hide behind some shrubbery when a car drives by.

Now I'm alone again, sitting on the curb in the darkened street, wondering what I should do next.

I remove Sara's phone from my back pocket and stare at the notification for a long time.

Why would a woman like Sara be writing to *him*?

Does this mean that @MrSugarDaddy111 *is* her husband? That she's been lying to me?

It's so messed up.

But it also doesn't make any sense. Sara has been so nice to me, wanting to help. Offering me cash…

Oh shit. Then it hits me.

Maybe she knows what happened to my sister. Maybe she's in on it and is being nice because she feels guilty.

I shiver, even though I'm wearing a hoodie.

If this is the case, if Sara is involved, then this whole world is just a shitty place to be in, and I'm glad my sister is in a better place.

No, that's not true. I'll never be glad about Dani being

gone. I miss her so much. It hurts every morning when I wake up and remember that she's dead.

The phone feels heavy in my hands. I'm surprised that Sara doesn't have the latest iPhone. But then I recall what she told me about her past. She's not some princess who's had everything gifted to her on a silver platter. She's been through stuff.

Though I don't want to do it, as it feels so wrong to betray Sara after she's been so nice to me, I punch in the passcode and unlock the phone.

She probably didn't believe me when I said I memorise strangers' passcodes while I'm washing car windows.

I click on the message. It's a direct message on Instagram, just like the ones my sister was receiving.

I start from the beginning, which isn't too far to scroll back to. Sara only started talking to this person a little over an hour ago.

Weird.

So she doesn't know him then?

I read on.

A bit of sexy talk, which is embarrassing to read. It's kind of hard to believe that Sara would speak to a guy like this.

It almost seems like she's... into him. Or at least pretending she's into him.

She calls herself @MissSugarBaby007, which again, is not what I imagine Sara would call herself online.

I nearly drop the phone when I scroll down to a very blurry picture of... oh crap, Sara sent *this?*

I shake my head and try my best not to look at it, and instead focus on the next few messages, which are the arrangements they've made to meet up.

I check the time on the phone and realise that they are meeting right this minute.

Why would Sara do this?

Then it hits me. And I feel like such an idiot for not

realising sooner.

She's not meeting him because she's got a thing for sugar daddies.

Sara is just as curious as me as to who is behind her husband's photo.

Shit.

I jump to my feet.

She's at that hotel now, with a potential murderer.

I need to go to the police with this.

Then I remember the card that the younger cop who visited our house gave me, in case I heard anything about my sister.

I take it out of my wallet and dial him up.

But I end the call before it picks up.

I've got a stolen phone. What if they lock me up for this?

But it only takes me a few seconds to decide that Sara's life is worth it.

Even if they lock me up, at least they'll know where she is, and they can get their hands on this man and drag him in for questioning.

My heart pounds while I wait for the police to answer.

Every minute, every second is vital.

Who knows what that psycho could be doing to Sara?

The cop finally answers.

'Hello, Detective Hugal, how can I help?'

My throat locks up, and for about half a minute, I say nothing.

The sound of paper being shuffled in the background fills the silence.

'Sara Kingston?' he says, and I'm shocked that he knows it's her phone.

'Umm, no... it's Harley. Harley Stokes.'

'Harley? What are you doing with Sara Kingston's phone?'

'How did you know it was her number?'

Detective Hugal is quiet for a moment. 'I can't divulge that.'

I guess he may have gotten it after questioning her husband. They were probably planning on asking her a few questions at some point.

My heart is thumping so loud I wonder if he can hear it through the phone.

'Sara's in trouble.'

'What kind of trouble? Listen, can you stay where you are, Harley? I'll come to speak to you. Are you home?'

'No. I'm not.' I glance at the nearby street sign and give him the address.

'I'm coming. Do not leave, please, Harley. Can you promise me that?'

'I promise,' I say.

I can't stop thinking about Sara in that hotel room, alone with whoever that psycho is. The lengths she is going to, just to find out who is behind that account. I know she wants to clear her husband's name, to get whoever it is that is using his image, but I also think she has the same suspicions as me. That whoever is behind that account murdered my sister.

It takes the detective only three minutes to get here, and I wonder if he broke the law and sped to get to me.

'Get in,' he says, his face both serious and compassionate.

Once I'm in the car, I put on my seat belt. It smells like coffee in here and there's a digital screen with a lot of buttons and a radio going, not with music, but with static conversations between police officers.

'Now tell me how you came into possession of Sara's phone,' Detective Hugal says, his brows raised.

I explain exactly what happened.

'So you stole it, Harley?'

'I did. But look.' I unlock the phone and hold it out

between us. 'Look. Read this for yourself,' I say. 'Click on Instagram and go to the direct messages.'

He does and I wait for his face to change, but it doesn't.

'There's nothing here. Her DMs are empty.'

'Wait.' I look at the phone. He's right. They're gone. But I know what I saw. I'm not going insane.

'Harley,' Detective Hugal says, his voice dripping with pity. It makes me so angry I want to break the radio and shut those voices out, make him listen to me and take me seriously.

'It was there. She went to the ATM to get me some cash out, for my sister's funeral. I waited for her, because I know how much that money would mean to my parents. But then a notification popped up on her screen. It was from @MrSugarDaddy111.'

Detective Hugal gives me a long look.

'Are you sure?'

'Yes. I saw it. Why the hell would I make this up? Then I unlocked the phone and read the whole lot. They're meeting at a hotel, and I'm worried about her.' I shrug. 'The guy must have deleted his account or blocked her or deactivated it or something, because the messages were there a few minutes ago.'

'Do you know Sara personally?' the detective asks, frowning in confusion. 'Is she a relation of yours? Or a family friend?'

'Give me the phone back,' I say. 'We're wasting time. Sara could be getting hurt.'

The detective sighs.

'No. It's police property now. I'll have to go to Sara's house, explain what happened and give it back to her.'

'But I saw the messages. She's not going to be home. She's meeting him now at room 58, at the Hotel... Stan... something. Stanford or Stanton. Stanton, that's it. You need to go there now. Right now.'

Detective Hugal's face turns serious and for a second,

I feel like he's going to take me seriously.

But then he says, 'I'm going to drop you home, Harley.'

I put my hands on the car door, threatening to run.

'No. I'm not going anywhere until I know you're going to take me seriously. That you're going to check this out for me.' Tears prickle my eyes and I blink them away. I don't want the detective to see how upset I'm getting.

'Look at me, Harley,' he says, his voice calm.

I don't look at him. I just continue to stare out the passenger window at the house we're idling in front of.

'I'll drop you home and go straight to the hotel to investigate. How about that?'

After some thought I nod. It's the best that I can hope for.

When he pulls into my driveway, I get out and lean over the open passenger window to speak to him.

'Go straight there,' I say.

He puts up a hand, pausing our conversation while he speaks to someone on the radio, something about a hold-up at a petrol station. Great. I know what this means.

'I'm on my way,' he says into the radio hand speaker.

'What is it? Are you going to get Sara?'

He looks at me. 'I've got work to do, Harley,' he says. 'But I'll check it out. Leave it with me. I'm sure Sara is fine.'

He pulls out, turns on his lights and sirens and speeds off into the night.

I know he's going to the stupid petrol station robbery, because I heard him say 'I'm on my way'.

Right now, Sara is in a hotel room with God knows who, and I feel partly responsible for getting her into this mess.

Shit. Shit. Shit.

I know Sara has her own reasons for going there

tonight, but I can't just leave her there to face whoever it is all alone.

She doesn't even have her phone with her, no thanks to me.

My house is dark. Mum and Dad and Selina are asleep, or at least trying to sleep. I don't think any of us has slept a proper night since Dani died.

I know I should go inside my house like Detective Hugal told me to, but instead I turn away and start running.

I'm not sure how long it will take me to run to Hotel Stanton, but I don't care.

I'll run the whole way if it means getting to Sara on time.

I just pray that she's okay.

That she's still alive.

35

Sara

'What did you do to her?' I say, tugging at my handcuffed wrist even though I know I can't free myself.

'Who?' he says, barely acknowledging me while he stares at his phone. 'Nice breasts by the way, Sars.'

I jangle the handcuff against the bedrail again. The metal digs painfully into my skin.

'You know exactly who I'm talking about. The murdered girl. Danielle Stokes.'

He stiffens when I say her name and puts down his

phone, then turns to me, his nostrils flaring, his cheeks inflamed.

'You think you're so smart,' he says, shaking his head. '@MissSugarBaby007. Really? You think you're a bit of a detective, don't you? But really, you're just a nosy bitch, Sara. You can't keep your fucking nose out of my business, can you? You can't keep your nose out of anyone's business. Always suspicious of things, always asking questions and wanting to know every fucking detail.'

As his rage builds, he begins to tremble. It scares the hell out of me.

Where on earth is Bethany with that bottle of champagne? It's been at least ten minutes, possibly more, since I was dragged into the room and cuffed to the bed.

Though I fought and scratched his face, I was useless against his brute strength, and after he bent my arms behind my back, I nearly passed out from the pain.

'How long have you been doing this for?' I ask, as casually as possible, because if I keep him talking, then perhaps it'll buy me time until Bethany gets here. 'This daddy thing?'

He shrugs. 'I don't know, a few months,' he says, grinning. 'Why, you interested in becoming a sugar mamma? You want tips?'

I roll my eyes at him. It must have been the wrong thing to do, because his grin vanishes as quickly as it had come.

'Look at you, Little Miss Judgy. Little Miss "I'm such a poor and dirty bitch, I need free soup, and oh I'll take one slice of bread and a side of rich husband with it".'

He snorts and looms over me.

'You're no better. Who's to know if you were truly living on the streets? What if you used your little sob story just to get our sympathy?' He wags his index finger at me. 'Sara, Sara, do we really know you? The real you? You're probably a scammer for all we know.'

'Stop trying to make this about me,' I say, getting my back up at his suggestion. As if I'd fake sleeping it rough and beg for free soup if I didn't need to. It's very typical of someone like him to question my background. Someone who has lived a privileged life and has never had to wonder where their next meal is coming from.

'Okay, scammer,' he says, grinning again.

'Please,' I say. 'You're the only fake artist in this room. For years... acting like you care about the homeless and people less fortunate than you. When really you don't care about anyone except yourself. You're sadistic. A pervert.'

His face reddens again, darker this time.

'Shut your trap.'

'The truth hurts, doesn't it? I wonder how you'll feel when people find out what you did to that poor girl?'

He seems confused for a moment.

'Wait,' I say. 'You're acting like there's more than one. That you're unsure who I'm talking about?'

He sits on the edge of the bed and reaches for the whisky on the bedside table and takes a swig.

'Only one got hurt. I'm not a monster, Sara.'

I keep my face neutral, and my mouth shut. There's no telling what sets this guy off.

'She was a sweet girl,' he says quietly. 'At least, I thought she was. But she looked at me like you did just now. Like I was a lesser being. That she was better than me. A poor piece of trash and she looked at me like *I* was the dirt. I could see it in her eyes. Her eyes literally said, "He's not good enough for me, so I'd better get this over with so I can get out of here." I could clearly see the disgust on her face.'

'Did she?'

'Did she what?' He takes a huge gulp and finishes the rest of the booze then flops back against the bed, his head resting against my thigh. It makes my skin crawl to have any part of his body touch mine.

'Did she get out of here... the room, alive?'

He arches his back, so that he can look at me, his face upside down. From this angle, he looks like the devil with his red face and bloodshot eyes.

I'm completely taken aback when tears well in his eyes.

'It wasn't this hotel. It was another one. A trashy one. But I can't go back there anymore. I've been using this one ever since.' He shakes his head from side to side, his hair brushing against my leg. 'But she's the only one I hurt. The only one that... went wrong.'

I can barely breathe. But I want to keep him talking.

'So did she leave that place alive?'

He sighs and rolls over so that he can look me in the eye, his chin digging into my thigh.

'What if I tell you that she didn't? That I'm the monster you think I am?'

I inhale sharply but try not to allow my face to betray my emotions.

'I'd feel awful, for her and for you. Because it must have been horrible.'

'Sure you would,' he says, scoffing. 'You and your high horse. You've always looked down your nose at me. Even though I'm the one with the money and you're the street trash.'

'No,' I say, keeping my voice even and calm, because I realise that Bethany must have forgotten me, and now I have no way out of this situation other than by keeping him as calm as possible.

'I haven't ever thought bad of you. I've always thought the best of you. You know that.'

He blinks and the tears dribble down his cheeks, soaking into my leggings.

'You're lying,' he says and in one swift move, he raises his head slightly and chomps down on my thigh.

I scream.

He releases me and rises to his knees, clamping a sweaty hand over my mouth.

'Shut up! Shut up or I'll strangle you right here, right now.'

His fingers smell like whiskey. I nod my head, maintaining eye contact until he removes his hand.

'Okay. And if I do keep quiet,' I say, doing my best to keep my breathing even, 'what will you do? Let me go?'

He gently strokes my hair and tucks the loose strands behind my ears.

'Let you go?' He shakes his head. 'That can't happen. You'll tell everyone and nobody will look at me with respect anymore. My parents, my friends... you. No. No. No. You'll have to be shut up eventually,' he says, stroking my chin. 'It's just, I need to work out how.'

He glances around the room and gnaws on his bottom lip. 'This place isn't like the motel where I met that girl. It was easier to get away with what I did there. At a place where no one cares.'

He slides his hand, featherlight, from the tip of my chin down to my neck, where he applies pressure against my windpipe using his thumb. Just when I start to panic, thrashing my arms and legs, the handcuffs jangling noisily against the bedframe, he snorts and lets me go.

'The look on your face, Sars,' he says, practically choking on his laugh while I choke on my breath and gasp for air. 'This is going to be a fun night, @MissSugarBaby007.'

36

Neve

As I struggle to open my eyes, the first thing I notice is how heavy my head and limbs feel, as though I weigh a tonne. My tongue feels wrong too. Thick and dry. I'm in desperate need of some water to drink.

I roll onto my side and my hips dig into the cold, hard ground beneath me.

Where am I?

I blink under the dim glow of the single flickering globe in the ceiling above me.

The room around me appears foreign at first. But as my eyes adjust to the dimness, I spy some familiar things. A framed enlarged photo of my husband's first car. I got him this for his thirtieth birthday. Then there's the television set-up with the Xbox console, and the gaming chair in the corner of the room.

I'm in the cellar of my own house. My husband's man cave.

Who did this to me?

But no matter how hard I think, I cannot recall anybody grabbing me and forcing me in here.

Was it Stan? Surely not. Why on earth would he hurt me?

Lawrence?

Though my head spins when I move, I manage to get on my feet.

Have I been drugged?

Swaying, I stagger to the door and try the handle. Of course it is locked. I bang on it several times.

'Stan?'

I'm not sure what time it is. Or if Jake is home or at school.

Then it hits me.

What if Jake is in trouble? What if somebody has broken in and has thrown me in here while they attack my boy?

Liv comes to mind. Dear Liv.

And then a memory strikes my mind, like a bolt of lightning.

Liv.

I was looking for information on Liv.

The phone company said that her number was no longer connected, so I looked on Stan's phone, while he went to the toilet. He had it open on the bathroom countertop... and I saw some texts he'd sent her.

On her *new* number.

A fresh stab of hurt pierces my heart as I recall what I saw.

Why would Liv have sent her new number to Stan but not me?

I try to remember what some of the messages she'd sent him contained but can only seem to recall snippets.

> *You didn't send me the whole lot*
> *You promised*
> *She's horrible... I'm so sorry, Dad.*
> *London is good. I think I'll stay here for a while. But I miss Jakey.*

My pulse thunders in my ears. I feel so faint that I need to steady myself against the locked cellar door.

Oh my God.

Liv is in *London.* And Stan has known all along?

My head begins to pound and my knees buckle.

Why is Liv in London? Why won't she speak to me? What was she sorry to Stan about? Did she mean *me* when she wrote 'she's horrible'?

I slide down to the cold, hard ground and spend the next minute or so trying to make sense of all of this, when I hear a sound coming from somewhere above me.

Though it's faint, it's unmistakable. Somebody is knocking on the front door of my house.

'I'm here,' I shout. 'Help!'

The knocking continues.

I drag myself to my feet and stagger over to the only window in this room. It's a small window, which is at ground level, where our roses grow in the front yard. It has steel bars across it, but I can maybe poke something through and smash the narrow pane or at the very least make a sound.

It's dark outside and I can hear crickets singing. How long have I been down here for?

I shake my head. I need to concentrate on getting out of here.

You'd think a man cave would have useful things like tools inside of it, but as I scan the countertops and go through each drawer, I slam them shut in frustration when I realise there are none. Only a few pens, some magazines that I refuse to touch, and a few USB sticks.

The only thing that can potentially fit through the gaps of the window bars is the Xbox controller.

I grab it, yank the cord out from the back and stagger my way to the window.

Then I notice that the knocks on my front door have ceased and my heart stutters in panic.

Don't leave, please don't leave.

My first attempt as smashing the window produces only a dull thud, but my second attempt manages to smash through the glass, breaking it into shards.

'Help!' I scream through the broken window,

carefully stretching my now bleeding wrist through the small gap so that I can wave my hand and toss the Xbox controller. 'Help!'

Footsteps crunch against the lawn, drawing closer. Soon a shadow looms over me, blocking out the light from the streetlamp.

I scream when someone bends and puts their face to the gap.

'Oh my God, Neve,' he says, his eyes wide.

The look of horror in his kind eyes makes me want to cry, and as I touch my aching, bruised face, I finally remember, with horror, the person who did this to me.

37

Edward

'Is there another way in?' I ask Neve, who, through the broken cellar window, I can see crying, her face a swollen mess of bruises.

'You need to get in through the house. The cellar door can be unlocked from the garage. Smash a window. Please. Hurry. I don't know where Jake is. I think Stan did this to me.'

'Stan?' I freeze for a split second, the shock of hearing that Neve is hurt at the hands of her own husband, my best friend, rendering me momentarily speechless. 'Are you sure it wasn't Lawrence?'

She frowns in confusion, tears shining in her eyes. 'I don't know. I don't remember.'

I'd come here looking for Stan. Because I wanted to ask him why in hell he called my parents to talk shit about me behind my back, and also, more importantly, I want to speak to him about the young woman I'd seen him with at the hotel, the work colleague. The one who I overhead call him 'sugar daddy'. I wanted to ask him if he was the person behind the Instagram account who used my photo. The account that was talking to that girl, Danielle Stokes.

Stan had access to that picture. It was Neve who took it when we all went on holiday to Melbourne. But he hasn't been answering my messages or my calls. I even threatened him with going to the police if he didn't get back to me within the hour.

But there's no time to waste on thoughts of Stan. Neve needs my help. Potentially Jake too.

'Okay. I'm coming in,' I say, before I rise to my feet and select a decent-sized rock from the front garden.

I walk around the house and spy the laundry window. The curtains are open, so I can see that the room is empty. The last thing I'd want is for Jake to get hurt if he's still inside.

Here goes.

I toss the rock at the glass, and it immediately shatters into shards. The remaining few pieces smash to the ground as I kick them away and enter the house. I'm surprised that the alarm system hasn't gone off, but Stan may have turned it off himself so that Neve couldn't trigger it while she was trapped in the cellar.

'Jake,' I call, but after a quick search from room to room, there doesn't appear to be anybody inside the house.

I head straight to the garage.

'Neve!'

I try the cellar door handle, but of course it's locked.

'Neve,' I shout at the door.

After a while I hear a sound, shuffling, then she

pounds on the door weakly with her fists.

'Eddie! Is Jake okay?'

'He's not here. I called out and took a quick look around.'

Neve says nothing for a while, but I can hear her sob.

'Neve. We need to get you out so that we can find Jake.'

'There's a key hanging on the hook beside that old credenza, near where I park my car,' she says.

I spy the empty hook and swear.

'There's a hook, but no key.'

'Oh God,' she says. 'He must have taken it with him.'

Adrenaline rattles through my veins, making me jog on the spot.

'I'm going to have to kick it open, Neve. Stand back.'

'I'm out the way. You can do it now,' she says, her voice further away.

'Okay, I'm coming,' I shout, before I rear back and kick the door right near the handle. It creaks and I manage to damage the door a little, cracking the wood, but it doesn't open.

'I'm trying again.'

This time, I stand right back, grateful that Stan's car isn't in the garage, and bolt towards the door, using my shoulder to bash against it.

It opens, and I fly into the cellar, landing on the cool concrete with a thud that sends pain shooting up my shoulder.

Neve comes to my side and helps me to stand. She's wobbly on her feet herself and after I've got my bearings, I'm the one supporting her.

'What happened to you? Who do you think did this?'

'I don't know. Stan, I think. It has to be Stan. I think I've been drugged,' she says, her hand lightly touching her forehead, 'because everything is foggy.' She gingerly touches her bruised cheek and jaw. 'I honestly didn't even know I'd been hurt until you looked at me through the window. I could tell by the look on your face that it was bad.'

'So you can't be sure that Stan did this then?'

'I'm not sure now,' she says, as I lead her out the cellar and into the garage. 'It's all a blur.'

'Let's get you out of here,' I say.

'We'll go in your car,' she says. 'There's no time to waste. Are you sure Jake isn't inside?'

I shake my head. 'I called out and searched.' I nod to the empty verge, where Lawrence's car was parked the last time Sara and I were here. 'Looks like Lawrence isn't home either.'

Neve turns pale and takes out her phone to make a call.

'Hi, Mum ... No ... Oh. That's good. So everything is okay.' She sighs with relief. 'Oh, so Jake is enjoying his time with you. That's so good ... Okay. I'll pick him up in a couple of hours or so. I've just got something to do ... Don't let him out of your sight, please. And don't let Stan pick him up. I will be doing that. Just keep the door locked until I get there ... I'm sorry, I can't explain now. Tell Jake I love him, and that I'll see him a bit later ... Love you, Mum ... Thank you.'

She hangs up.

'Mum said that Stan dropped Jake off earlier today. He told her I was feeling sick and asked if she could watch Jake.'

'At least he's safe,' I say.

'True. But I can't say the same about Liv.' Neve looks me dead in the eye. 'She's in London, Eddie.'

'London? But Sara told me you were in Melbourne looking for her?'

'Melbourne?'

'Yeah. You sent her a text a few hours ago... oh, wait... oh shit.' I sigh when it dawns on me. 'That must have been Stan who wrote that.'

Neve nods. 'Stan's been telling lots of lies.' She raises

a trembling hand to her throat as tears fill her eyes. 'I just hope... I just hope that nobody gets hurt,' she says, swallowing thickly. 'Or that he hasn't hurt anyone already.'

'You mean Danielle Stokes, don't you?'

She inhales sharply, then nods.

I help Neve into the passenger seat of my car and then climb in, but I don't start the car just yet.

'So how much do you remember? How can you be certain that Stan did this to you and not Lawrence?'

She touches her face again and she sighs.

'I was checking his phone, while he was in the toilet. I wanted to see if he'd heard from Liv. If he was keeping things from me. Because he's been acting weird.'

'Had he heard from Liv?'

'Yes. As I said, she's in London. I don't remember everything I saw, exactly, but she said something like "she's horrible" and "sorry, Dad". That kind of thing. I think she means me.'

'What? That doesn't sound right... and why would Stan keep this from you?'

'Your guess is as good as mine.' She put a hand to her lips, as though she's suddenly remembered something. 'Oh God, then I accused him of sleeping with the dead girl. Because he'd gone out to meet someone that night, the night they say she was murdered. And he's normally gone for two hours max. But this time, he didn't get back until 3am. And he was so cold when he returned. I think his clothes may have been wet, the pants had a funny line along the ankles, as though he'd been standing in water, and his shoes smelt putrid the next day,' she says, her nose wrinkling at the memory.

'Did you ask him where he'd been?'

'Yeah. He gave me some story about his colleague getting bogged and having to push him out. Said the man wanted to take us both out to dinner next month to thank us. It all sounded so believable.'

'So what makes you think he was lying about that?'

She's quiet for a long time.

'Stan's been sleeping with other women, Eddie.'

I sigh, feeling terrible for Neve.

'I know. I saw him one night. I know I should have told you but... I promised him. He said that it was the last time.'

'Oh, don't worry. I know all about it. But the affairs aren't what I'm worried about.' Neve winces and tentatively touches her swollen cheek. 'I asked him, yesterday, if that dinner with his colleague was still happening, the one he supposedly helped out after he'd gotten bogged.' Tears fill Neve's eyes. 'And you know what? He didn't even know what I was talking about. Said I was making things up. So I know he's lying about where he was that night. The night the girl was supposed to have been murdered.'

My blood runs cold. Stan is my best mate. I've known him all my life. He wouldn't ever hurt someone. He doesn't have it in him.

'Anyway, back to today. As I said I was checking his phone one minute, and then I woke up in the cellar, my brain foggy with drugs. He did something to me, drugged me and then threw me in here. Maybe things got rough,' she says, touching her jaw. 'I think the tea he's been making for me... it tastes funny. I think he's been putting something in it.'

'I'm so sorry, Neve,' I say. 'I've been a shitty friend. I was so wrapped up in my own, mine and Sara's issues, that I didn't even think...' I shake my head. 'I should have been there for you.'

I've known Neve since high school, for as long as I've known Stan. I should have been there for her.

Neve shrugs her petite shoulders.

'At least I now know where Liv is. And I know that he's responsible for keeping Liv and me apart. He's obviously told her lies to make her hate me.' Neve wipes her cheeks as more tears stream down her face. 'My Liv would never have flown overseas without saying goodbye to me, unless he told her some terrible lie.'

I put a hand to my forehead and release a sigh.

'I think I know what he's been telling Liv,' I say.

'What?'

'Stan told Sara that he thought you and I were having an affair, which is ridiculous of course. Sara refused to believe it by the way. So I can imagine he probably said something along those lines to Liv. In fact, it explains why Liv told Sara that she doesn't want anything to do with us anymore.' I shake my head. 'It actually explains a lot. But why on earth would Stan make something like that up?'

'I don't know. But at least there's hope now, of getting Liv back. She'll believe us if we all tell her the same thing.'

'You never know,' I say, not wanting to give her false hope.

After hearing all of this, I desperately want to call Sara and tell her everything. But I need to get Neve to hospital first, so that her injuries can be looked at. At least I know that Sara is safe at home with Carmella.

I start the car and ask Neve to buckle her seat belt. But when she doesn't, I glance at her and can see that she's shaking.

'What is it, Neve?'

'It's all my fault,' she says, her eyes staring off into space.

'It's nobody's fault. Stan's the one messing around with us all. If it's anyone's fault, it's Stan's.'

Neve shakes her head.

'I was the one who suggested he meet other women. That we have an open marriage. Not that I wanted to meet other men. I just wanted Stan to leave me alone for once. Maybe Liv found out about it. Maybe Stan was saving face by lying and saying that it was me that was sleeping around.' Neve snorts and shakes her head. 'I think he's been fucking Sondra across the street, too. I just know it. And God knows what he's been telling her because she absolutely hates me for no reason.'

I turn the car off and give my full attention to Neve.

'Did you know about the Instagram account? The daddy one? The one with my photo on it?' There's a desperation to my voice. I'm finally closer to the truth. 'Because the police took me in for questioning because of it. They thought I killed that girl. They thought I was the last person to speak with her.'

Her eyes widen and she puts a hand to her mouth.

'I helped upload the photo. I didn't want to, but he was so angry I just did what I was told,' she says. 'It was that picture of us four on that holiday in Melbourne, zoomed in at Stan's face. But the way it uploaded was all wrong. It got your face instead of Stan's. Stan got even more angry with me and told me he was going to fix it himself. But I guess he didn't.' She blinks and looks me in the eye. 'Oh God, I'm so sorry, Eddie.'

'It's done now,' I say, feeling pissed off in general, but not wanting to cause her any more distress. 'It's okay.'

'But it's not okay. If I hadn't pushed Stan to see other women, to give me a break from his demanding sexual needs, then he wouldn't have started talking to that poor girl.'

'We don't know for sure if Stan did anything to hurt her, though. Let's not jump to conclusions. She could have met another man that night. We just don't know.'

Neve nods. 'But we need to go to the police right away. They need to know what's going on, that Stan is the one behind the account.'

I nod. 'And we need to take you to hospital.'

'Police first.'

'Okay, we'll tell the police first,' I say, keeping my voice steady. 'Then we'll go straight to hospital.'

I start the car and try to call Sara, but she doesn't

answer.

So I message her instead.

> *Sara, I'm with Neve. There are some things you need to know. Stay home with your mum and don't open the door to anyone, especially not Stan. He may be dangerous. I'll explain later.*

Thank God Carmella is at home with Sara. It makes me feel a little bit better about not being with my wife right now.

At least I know that she's safe.

38

Officer Hugal

There hasn't been a second to think about Harley and Sara, especially not while I was busy detaining the perpetrator from the robbery at the petrol station.

But now that I'm back in my car, Sara's phone lights up, reminding me of my promise to Harley to go to Hotel Stanton to check if she's there.

Something about that kid, a seriousness not usually found in teenage boys, warns me that he was telling me the truth.

I pick up the phone from the centre console and read the message. It appears to be from her husband, Edward, the one we had in for questioning, the one who provided both his and his wife's number should I require them both for further questioning.

His message is a little odd. He warns her to stay indoors and to not open the front door for anyone, especially not Stan. Who is Stan? Someone dangerous enough for Sara's husband to warn her about, that's for certain.

Harley's face flashes before my eyes. The tears in the poor kid's eyes. I can't let him down. He's already lost his sister.

I shake my head and put my car into gear and start to drive in the direction of Hotel Stanton.

I just hope I'm not too late.

39

Liv

London is amazing. It truly is. I feel as though I need to pinch myself every morning when I wake up, because I almost can't believe that I'm here.

'Liv, *hello*?'

Something warm slaps my face and I can't help but smile when my new friend, Janine, grins at me from across the café booth table, waving her pancake.

'Sorry. I was just... thinking,' I say. 'And did you just slap me with a pancake?'

She laughs. 'Are you missing home, too?' she asks, her playful expression turning serious. Janine is from New Zealand, so we're basically considered cousins over here.

My stomach turns as I stare at my plate of bacon and eggs, which by now is getting cold. I decide instead to sip my tea.

'No way,' I say, after I've swallowed a few mouthfuls of tea. 'I'm glad to be as far away from my family as possible.'

Janine drops her pancake onto her plate and raises a single eyebrow. 'I think you need to talk about it. It's not good keeping family issues locked away like that. Seriously, this comes from a place of experience. My mum is a school counsellor. I'm pretty much her protégée.'

I shrug and wonder what it would be like to have a normal family like Janine has. A normal mum who doesn't sleep around with your godfather.

'I can't talk about it yet. Thanks for the offer, but...' I shake my head. 'I'm still trying to digest everything my dad told me about my mum. It's pretty... heavy going.'

Janine's phone lights up.

'Do you mind if I read this?' she asks, her eyes sparkling with happiness. 'Oh my God. It's Dylan!'

I roll my eyes and laugh. Dylan is the guy Janine hooked up with last night at a party we went to.

'Of course I don't mind.'

She reads the text and looks up at me. 'He wants to meet me for a coffee. Right now.'

'Oh wow, that's great,' I say, grinning at her.

'But I don't want to leave you if you're not feeling great,' she says, frowning.

'Um, are you insane? You need to go meet this guy right now,' I say, and wave a hand at her. 'I'm fine. Actually the time alone will do me good. I think I'll go to the library and do some reading, and maybe some thinking.'

'Okay,' she says, seemingly satisfied with my plans for the day, the pancakes she'd been drooling over only a few minutes ago forgotten now. 'But text me if you need me.'

'Will do,' I say, and smile to show how okay I am. 'You can tell me everything tonight over pizza on the couch.'

'One hundred percent,' she says, squealing.

When Janine is out of sight, I let my face fall and allow myself to drift off, back to the night everything changed. The night before my dad packed me off on a plane to the very grey and beautiful London.

I was walking home after a gatho at my friend's house. They live only a street away from ours, and I was taking a shortcut, a footpath which runs along the length of a small lake. Apparently before the housing development, it was known as a swamp, but you can't tell that to my parents or any of the other snobs who reside at Lakeland Gardens.

That night I was feeling shitty. There weren't many of my close friends at the party, because most of them had flown overseas to start their gap year and do the backpacker thing around Europe. And the only reason I wasn't over there with them was because my mum is a freak about me living away from home and wanted me to wait until I turned eighteen. That was back when things were good between Mum and me.

But anyway, I remember freaking out when I passed the lake and saw the silhouette of a man standing there, knee-deep. You always hear stories of girls getting attacked when they cut through parks or bushland, and here I was, alone with a man. Something my mother was always warning me about.

Then when he called my name, I nearly screamed, until I realised that it was my dad standing there.

After I got over the shock of seeing my dad standing in the middle of a swamp, I got close enough to see that his face was wet with tears. He'd been crying.

The whole situation gave me goosebumps and left

me feeling cold.

'Let's go home,' I said, trying to coax him out of the water. 'You'll feel better when you're home with Mum.'

But he just shook his head as the tears continued to stream down his face.

'Your mum won't want me anymore,' he said, groaning. 'She won't want me.'

'What are you talking about, Dad? Come on. Let's go home. You're sounding really weird. It's freaking me out.'

'Do I scare you, Liv?'

'What? No.' I slapped at a mosquito on my bare shoulder. 'It's late. Can we please go home?'

I didn't even want to ask him what he was doing here. I just wanted us both home, safe and sound. I wanted to be tucked into my bed, wearing my favourite pyjamas and snug under my doona.

'Your mum doesn't want me anymore.'

'What do you mean?' I asked. 'Is this why you're out here in the water?'

He thought about it, but then nodded.

'She... she's... having an affair.' He gestured towards the water. 'I want to kill myself. Yes,' he said again, as though convincing himself of the fact. 'I want it all to end.'

'Wait. Mum's having an affair?' The blood in my veins turned cold. Because I believe my dad. Because why else would he be standing out in the rank, stinking water. 'Oh my God. I'm so sorry, Dad. Are you sure?'

He nodded.

I stepped towards him, resisting the urge to scream when swamp water soaked into my favourite sneakers.

'Take my hand, Dad. I'll help you out and then we can go home and figure this out.'

Dad looked at me, his eyes wide and flickering with hope.

'I'll come out on one condition.'

Because I was so desperate to get my dad out of the water and home safe, where he couldn't try to drown himself, I nodded.

'Anything, Dad. Anything.'

He stared long and hard at the water.

'Don't tell anyone you saw me here. Not even your mother.'

'I promise.'

'Good,' he said. 'And then I want you to go home and then pack your bags for an overseas trip.'

'Pack my bags? Why?' I asked, my heart pounding furiously against my ribcage.

Dad's face looked yellow under the dim glow from the nearby streetlamp.

'Because I'm booking you a flight to London, Liv, to go be with your friends. And don't worry about money. I'll give you lots. More than you'll ever need.'

And now, here I am, in London.

It's been good for the most part. I've caught up with all my friends from home, and I've made such great new friends, like Janine.

But I can't help but worry about Dad.

Part of me wishes that I hadn't gotten a new phone. Because I can't remember my mother's number off by heart. Sometimes I want to call her and yell and scream at her for hurting my dad like that. Hurting him so much that he wanted to drown himself in a swamp.

But then, other times, when I remember how much she loves me, I'm glad that I don't have a phone. Because deep down, even though I'm mad at her for having an affair, I don't hate her, and I don't want her hurt.

I just want to tell her that I miss her, and that I love her. Because I still do.

I just want everything to be okay, again.

I want my family back.

But that's not going to happen anytime soon. Not if Mum has been sleeping with Edward. And even if they stopped their affair, nothing will ever be the same again.

At least here, on the other side of the globe, I can pretend that everything is okay.

40

Harley

I slow down when I get to the hotel entrance and catch my breath. They'll kick me out if I run inside all puffed and sweaty.

The night air cools my body as I walk around with my arms up and flap my hoodie around myself. I hope I don't smell too bad. I didn't get a chance to shower today, with everything that happened.

When my breathing is controlled again, I tidy my hair and tuck the loose strands behind my ears and take a deep breath before I enter the hotel through the sliding doors.

It smells nice in here, and the place looks so clean. There are pretty flowers everywhere. I can't imagine anything bad happening here. So I hope I'm wrong about Sara being in danger.

There's a young, twenty-something girl at the counter, she's dressed in the hotel uniform, but she looks like she's about to remove her name badge. Maybe she's finished for the night. I'd better catch her before she leaves.

'Hi. Have you seen my... my mum?' I lie. 'She came in nearly an hour ago. She was wearing a brown cardigan and she has dark brown hair.'

The girl stares at me for a long moment and I wonder if she understood a word I said.

'She's staying in room 58,' I say, hoping it will jog her memory.

The girl puts a hand over her mouth.

'Oh my God,' she says. 'The champagne!'

She turns and eyes a nearby trolley. It's got a perspiring bucket of ice on it with a fancy-looking bottle buried inside.

A man clears his throat behind me, and I step aside. He has dark circles beneath his eyes, and he rests his briefcase against the counter and looks at the girl behind the desk wearily. 'Can I get a room, please?'

She glances at the trolley and then at me.

'That's for room 58,' she says. 'For your mum.'

'I can take it up to her, if you like,' I say. 'She's expecting me anyway.'

The girl glances at the tired businessman and then back at me.

'Okay,' she says, before lowering her voice. 'But be quick. Try not to let any of the other staff see you.' She shakes her head and mutters something about her shift being over a long time ago.

I quickly push the trolley across the lobby towards the elevators, before she changes her mind.

At the third floor I get out and push the trolley along the long, winding corridor, making a jangling noise as I go, until I reach number 58.

At the door I pause. Is Sara in this room? Is the person who murdered my sister in here? Just the idea of it makes me want to vomit or pass out.

Is the person going to hit me over the head with a blunt object? Something hard?

Because that's how my sister died.

A single blow to the back of her head. Enough to kill her instantly. She wouldn't have even known it had happened, according to Detective Hugal. He was trying to make us feel better about it, but it didn't. No one wants to picture their loved one getting hit that hard.

The key card for the room is resting against the ice bucket. With shaking hands, I pick it up and before I can stop myself, swipe it through, just like I've seen people do in the movies.

The little light beneath the door handle flickers green, and I nearly crap myself, but I draw in a deep breath and open it anyway.

I wonder if whoever is inside can hear me come in.

But the thought doesn't stop me.

I enter, and creep along the narrow corridor of the room, passing the open door of a bathroom. The towels are still rolled up and unused, and I can smell something… stale booze in the air.

The television is on, flickering shapes across the walls, but as I move deeper into the room, I catch sight of a bed, and of two pairs of legs, a woman's and a man's, entangled on top of white sheets.

The woman's legs are kicking out and my heart races when I realise that she is fighting him.

As I edge closer, abandoning the trolley, I can see that a man is holding the woman down, and that he's got his hands wrapped around her throat, squeezing the life out of her.

Sara. He is choking Sara, and they are both fighting so hard that neither of them has noticed me.

For a minute I'm struck dumb and don't know what to do, but then I spy an empty bottle of whisky and I carefully wrap my fingers around its neck.

Summoning up all the rage I've felt since the day I found out my sister died, I raise it up high over the man's head and smash it down hard.

41

Sara

Stan slumps against me and I use all the strength I have left in me to roll him off.

'Harley,' I say, my throat hoarse from Stan trying to kill me.

'Are you okay?' he asks. His skin is as pale as the walls and he's shaking all over. 'Did I kill him?'

'No. Don't worry about him. You need to get the keys,' I say, pointing to the top of the minibar, where Stan left them, 'and unlock me so we can get out of here before he wakes up.'

Harley grabs the keys and rushes to my side. After a bit of fumbling, he manages to unlock the cuffs and free me.

'Thank you, Harley,' I say, as he helps me to my feet.

'Let's move,' I say, my heart hammering against my chest. 'Hurry.'

But before we get to the door, Stan groans and suddenly, I'm knocked off my feet and Harley cries out from behind me.

When I look up, Stan has his arms around Harley, in a tight headlock.

'Don't hurt him,' I shout, rising to claw at Stan's arms.

Stan gives me a look that turns my blood cold as he yanks a struggling Harley from out of my reach.

'One twist, and he's dead,' he says, putting his other

hand to the side of Harley's head. 'I can snap his reedy little neck in seconds. So back the fuck away.' He shakes his head and raises his brows. 'He's her brother, isn't he? I recognise him from her photos.' He shakes his head again. 'You really are fucking nosy, aren't you, Sars? Getting cosy with my murder victim's family.' He tightens his grip on Harley.

'You don't want to do this, Stan. This isn't you,' I say, taking a step back.

Stan laughs. 'I nearly choked you to death a few minutes ago, but okay, "this isn't you". That's fucking hilarious, Sars.'

'Think of Neve,' I say, because I don't know what else to say and I'm clutching at straws. 'She loves you.'

'No she doesn't. She's repulsed by me. She's repulsed by my brother too.' He laughs. 'You know Lawrence is obsessed with Neve, right? My parents kicked him out of home when they found a painting of her in his bedroom. A painting of my wife, naked with her legs wrapped around my brother. Can you believe it?' Stan laughs. 'My mum clutched at her heart and fainted when she saw it. But I thought it was hilarious.'

'I saw Lawrence before. He was on my street in his car.'

'Probably trying to find Neve. I told him that she'd gone away, but he didn't believe me so I guess he must have gone to see if she was with you. To make sure that she was okay, that I hadn't hurt her.' Stan shrugs. 'My brother is a creepy stalker, what can I say. But he's a smart fucker. He started to work out that I may have been involved with the dead girl, so I threatened him. Told him that I'd tell Neve about him stealing her underwear if he said anything to anyone about it.'

I shudder. The brothers have more in common than I thought.

'What about Liv and Jake?' I say, trying to find something good and wholesome for Stan to cling to.

'You know they love you.'

Stan tightens his grip around Harley's neck, and I wince. Harley's dark eyes are starting to bulge, and his face has turned bright red.

'Liv won't love me anymore when she learns the truth. When she finds out I lied to her,' Stan says.

'What did you lie to her about?' I ask, edging close enough so that I can hold Harley's outstretched hand.

'She came across me in the water, when I was dumping that girl's body. Then I lied to her so she wouldn't know.'

Harley squeezes my fingers, and his eyes tear up. I squeeze him back. It hurts me that he has to hear about his sister like this, but I need to keep Stan talking, so that we can bide ourselves some time.

'What did you tell her?' I ask.

'I told her I was trying to kill myself because Neve was having an affair. It's the only thing I could think of at the time. It was after midnight. I was tired.'

'But Neve isn't having an affair.'

Stan pulls a face. 'Of course she isn't. And Eddie isn't either, by the way.' He rolls his eyes. 'I'll never be as perfect as your Eddie,' he spits. 'Of course precious Eddie would never do something like this. He's too busy gambling away your life savings. But I bet everyone still thinks he's an angel even when he fucks up, unlike me.'

'Gambling money is different to taking a life, Stan,' I say, at the risk of angering him. 'But you can get help. This is the moment you can change things. You can turn things around.'

Stan loosens his grip on Harley and my heart pounds in anticipation. He's going to let him go.

Harley squeezes my hand.

'Do you think Liv and Jake and Neve will forgive me? Even Eddie?'

'Of course. We'll all forgive you,' I say, holding tight to Harley's hand and moving closer.

'But, Neve... I've been so terrible to her. She started to work things out. I think she knew... she knew what I'd done. So I...' He shakes his head. 'Oh God, she'll hate me after this.'

'Neve loves you, Stan. You know that.'

Stan nods and loosens his hold on Harley a little more. Harley starts to breathe more evenly.

Stan's going to free him soon. I just know it.

But in that moment, the door bursts open and one of the police officers who took Edward in for questioning appears, gun in hand.

'Police!' he shouts. 'Don't move.'

My heart sinks. If he had showed up a few seconds later, I'd probably have Harley in my arms already.

'Stan. Please don't do anything rash,' I say. 'Remember what we spoke about. About turning things around?'

'Let the boy go,' shouts the officer.

Stan looks from me to the policeman, and he tightens his grip around Harley's neck and tugs him away from me, severing our joined hands.

'I've got nothing to lose,' he tells me, tears streaming down his cheeks. 'I may as well take someone else out before I go. Two siblings... that's pretty special.' He shrugs. 'Maybe I'll be remembered for it. Who knows? I might end up with my own Netflix original. Forever immortalised.'

'You don't need to involve the boy,' says the police officer, his voice calmer, softer. 'Let him go, or I'll shoot.'

'What if I want you to shoot me?' says Stan, shrugging. 'I've got nothing to live for anyway. You can shoot us both,' he says, laughing.

An idea comes to me, then. Something that may distract Stan. It's worth a shot.

While I keep my eyes glued to the stand-off in front of me, I slide my wedding band off my sweaty finger, then toss it against the mirror across the room.

The ring clangs against it noisily, just as I'd hoped, before it falls to the carpeted floor.

Stan flinches at the tinny sound and is distracted enough to loosen his grip on Harley so that I can tug him out of his arms.

Stan blinks and stares at me, his mouth open in surprise, before he lunges for us both, the broken neck of the whiskey bottle glinting in his hand.

A deafening crack fills the room.

Stan stumbles and then his gaze moves over the officer, then Harley, before he locks eyes with mine.

Blood blooms across his chest.

He opens his mouth, as though to speak, but before he can do so, he collapses to the floor, knocking his head against the end of the bed as he falls.

'Thank you,' I say to Harley, who sits on the edge of the bed, speechless, his eyes wide and fixed on Stan. 'Thank you for saving my life.'

He nods and his eyes fill with tears.

And I know what he's thinking.

He's wishing he could have saved his sister's life, too.

As I stare at Stan, the man I thought we all knew.

I wish the same.

Epilogue

Edith can't go on holiday overseas like she'd planned. Her doctor ruled against it. Her time is shorter than she initially thought.

So here we are, at the Beach Bar Café, enjoying the

apricot sunset after a day at the beach. Of course, most of the day was spent beneath an umbrella, with Edward, Jeoffrey and me making sure that Edith was coated in copious amounts of sunscreen because her skin is so sensitive after all the chemotherapy she received in the past. But it was still a lovely day.

'What a wonderful day,' Edith says, her green eyes glittering against the colours of the setting sun.

A waiter appears with a tray of French martinis.

Jeoffrey stands and takes the tray and hands the drinks out himself, passing Edith hers first, and then my mother's. Mum was invited to join us on the trip by Edith.

Once Edward and I have our drinks in hand, Jeoffrey raises his glass and toasts to another day well spent.

He's changed, Jeoffrey. Like all of us, he's learnt to live in the moment.

We don't know when Edith will be taken away from us, just like we don't know when any of us will leave.

And if the recent events have taught us anything, it's that we need to cherish every moment.

You can be here one minute and gone the next.

I raise my glass along with the others and then take a sip.

It's been three months since Stan was shot dead by that detective.

Three months since our lives were blown apart.

And while it's been difficult to process the loss of Stan, and the fact that he killed that innocent young girl, Danielle Stokes, life, as it always does, moves forward. It doesn't stop for anyone.

Edward and I are conscious now of how we spend our time and who we spend it with. We try not to waste it thinking about the past. And we've been giving more thought to what we want to do with our lives.

I've already enrolled in an online counselling course and Edward, along with the help of his parents, is in the process of starting a not-for-profit business that involves providing support to children experiencing grief and loss, whether through losing a loved one to an illness, such as cancer, or losing a loved one through an act of violence.

The recent events have helped us realise what it is we want to do.

Edward and I are excited.

We may not be able to have children of our own, but we can do our best to help as many kids as we can.

Edith is just as excited to be involved. She sees this work with children as something of a legacy she can leave behind. Something worthwhile she can do in her last moments here with us.

Edward wants to name the charity after his mother, but he doesn't want to do it now. 'She's not gone yet,' he told me late one night in bed. 'It doesn't feel right.'

Personally, I think he and Jeoffrey are secretly hoping that working on the charity will somehow miraculously heal Edith. But I don't blame them for that. A secret part of me hopes for this too, even though the rational side of me knows that it's unlikely.

Edith grows frailer and weaker with each day. And it's a great tragedy, to see such a beautiful, kind woman be robbed of her life so slowly and so cruelly.

But life is like that. It has its own agenda.

Liv is back from London. And although I know it's going to take a long time for Liv, Jake and Neve to heal, they've all asked to be a part of our charity organisation. To volunteer in any way that they can.

It's hard for the kids and Neve. Because they still love their version of Stan.

Neve's mum has come to stay with her, until she gets back on her feet, which has been a great help. And of course, we'll always be here for them.

Mum clinks her glass with mine, breaking me free of my thoughts.

I smile and take a sip and my fingers automatically reach for the golden acorn pendant resting against my chest – a gift from Edith, who, while fastening the delicate chain around my neck last night, thanked me for allowing her to realise her dream of passing the family heirloom on to her daughter, the daughter she had found in me.

'Are you okay, love?' Mum asks, as I blink my tears away.

I gaze at her aging face, at my in-laws, and my husband Eddie, and feel a rush of gratitude that we are all here together in this beautiful moment, the setting sun casting a soft golden light across our faces.

'Yes,' I say smiling. 'I am more than okay.'

The End

If you enjoyed this book, please let others know by leaving a quick review on Amazon. Also, if you spot anything untoward in the paperback, get in touch. We strive for the best quality and appreciate reader feedback.

editor@thebookfolks.com

Also by Vanessa Garbin

WHAT WE DID LAST NIGHT

When a group of close friends decide to hold a partner-swapping key party one night, it is meant to be "just a bit of fun". No obligations, but no strings attached. And anything that does happen will remain under wraps. But things quickly start to unravel, with utterly deadly consequences.

FREE with Kindle Unlimited and available in paperback!

THE LIES I TOLD HIM

When Daphne's teenage son returns from a party, distraught, he refuses to tell his mother what's up. But someone has filmed him in a compromising situation with a girl, and they are using it to get what they want. As Daphne tries to solve the problem, her own past comes back to haunt her and place everything she holds dear in jeopardy.

FREE with Kindle Unlimited and available in paperback!

YOUR EVERY MOVE

When young mother Dana discovers a bag of money under a bush, she thinks her problems may be over. Unfortunately, they are only just beginning. She starts to receive letters from someone claiming to be her "number one fan" and unless she complies with their bizarre demands, her family will be in danger.

FREE with Kindle Unlimited and available in paperback!

Other titles of interest

THAT MUCH SHE KNEW by Linda Hagan

A woman is found murdered. The same night, the office pathologist Jenny Norris goes missing. Worried that her colleague might be implicated, DCI Gawn Girvin in secret investigates the connection between the women. But Jenny has left few clues to go on, and before long Girvin's solo tactics risk muddling the murder investigation and putting her in danger.

FREE with Kindle Unlimited and available in paperback!

JOHN DEAN
THE GIRL IN THE
MEADOW
British crime fiction at its best

Sign up to our mailing list to find out about new releases and special offers!

www.thebookfolks.com

Made in United States
North Haven, CT
14 November 2022